SHARON SALA

is a child of the country. As a farmer's daughter, she found her vivid imagination made solitude a thing to cherish. During her adult life, she learned to survive by taking things one day at a time. An inveterate dreamer, she yearned to share the stories her imagination created. Sharon's dreams have come true, and she claims one of her greatest joys is when her stories become tools for healing.

JANIS REAMS HUDSON

is a prolific author of more than thirty-five novels, both contemporary and historical romances. Her titles have appeared on the bestseller lists of Waldenbooks, B. Dalton and BookRak, and have earned numerous awards, including a Reviewer's Choice award from *Romantic Times BOOKreviews* and National Reader's Choice Award. She's a three-time finalist for the Romance Writers of America's coveted RITA® Award, and is a past president of that ten-thousand member organization.

DEBRA COWAN

Like many writers, Debra made up stories in her head as a child. Her B.A. in English was obtained with the intention of following family tradition and becoming a schoolteacher, but after she wrote her first novel, there was no looking back. After years of working another job in addition to writing, she now devotes herself full-time to penning both historical and contemporary romances. An avid history buff, Debra enjoys traveling. She has visited places as diverse as Europe and Honduras, where she and her husband served as part of a medical-mission team.

Debra invites her readers to contact her at P.O. Box 30123, Coffee Creek Station, Edmond, Oklahoma 73003-0003, or via e-mail at her Web site at www.debracowan.net.

SHARON SALA
JANIS REAMS HUDSON
DEBRA COWAN

Aftershock

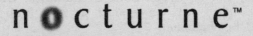

Silhouette Books

nocturne™

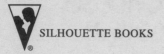

SILHOUETTE BOOKS

ISBN-13: 978-0-373-61796-8
ISBN-10:   0-373-61796-8

AFTERSHOCK

Copyright © 2008 by Harlequin Books S.A.

The publisher acknowledges the copyright holders
of the individual works as follows:

PENANCE
Copyright © 2008 by Sharon Sala

AFTER THE LIGHTNING
Copyright © 2008 by Janis Reams Hudson

SEEING RED
Copyright © 2008 by Debra Cowan

www.silhouettenocturne.com

Printed in U.S.A.

CONTENTS

PENANCE

Sharon Sala

Dear Reader,

Even at the worst of times, there is a positive to be found. We just have to look for it. When we've lost loved ones we think we can't bear to live without, there will be a friend who'll come shining through. During the most frightening of storms, we are given a rainbow. Through any kind of tragedy or loss, there will be one positive thing, even if it is just, "I have survived."

Such was the case for the heroine in my story, "Penance." Shot and left to die, she survived. Embarrassed by her surgery scars and her troubles with memory and mobility, she can't seem to see the positive in being alive, and focuses on what she's lost.

But then something begins to happen that she doesn't understand. What she first views as her penance for surviving becomes the most powerful gift she could have been given.

I hope when you read my story you take a moment to look into your own life and look past what you've lost to see what you have gained.

Be thankful for all that you have, and remember—there are people all over the world who would trade places with you in a heartbeat.

So, as I give you my story to read, I hope you enjoy the journey.

Sharon Sala

Life isn't fair. It's one of the first lessons we learn.
But life is precious, regardless of what
we endure to live it.

I believe that the people who come and
go throughout our lifetime are meant
to do so for a purpose.

Some teach us a lesson.

Some give us joy.

And some appear for the sole reason of showing us
the way life should be lived.

I call those people our angels.

I have had many angels in my life, and each
and every one has been an influence as to the
woman I have become.

I want to dedicate this book to my newest angel.

To Erin McClune.

Live every day with joy.

Chapter 1

October—New York City

Nicole Masters was sitting cross-legged on her sofa while a cold, autumn rain peppered against the windows of her fourth-floor apartment. She was poking at the ice cream in her bowl and trying not to be in a mood. The past few weeks had been life-changing in a very negative way, which was making it difficult for her to stay upbeat.

Six weeks ago, a simple trip to her neighborhood pharmacy had turned into a nightmare. She'd walked into the middle of a robbery. She never even saw the man who shot her in the head and left her for dead. She'd survived, but some of her senses had not. She was dealing with short-term memory loss and a tendency to stagger. Even though she'd been told the problems were most likely temporary, she waged a daily battle with depression.

Her parents had been killed in a car wreck when she was twenty-one. They'd owned the apartment building in which she had grown up, so finances were never going to be a problem. But she was alone. There were no aunts. No cousins. No grandparents. Except for a few friends—and most recently her boyfriend, Dominic Tucci, who lived in the apartment right above hers—she was alone. Her doctor kept reminding her that she should be grateful to be alive, and on one level, she knew he was right. But he wasn't living in her shoes.

If she'd been anywhere else but at that pharmacy when the robbery happened, then she wouldn't have died twice on the way to the hospital. She wouldn't be mistaking salt for sugar. She wouldn't be missing a head of hair and staggering like a drunk when she stood up. Instead of being grateful that she'd survived, she couldn't quit thinking of what she'd lost.

But that wasn't the end of her troubles. On top of everything else, something strange was happening inside her head. She'd begun to hear odd things. Sounds, not voices—at least, she didn't think it was voices. It sounded more like the distant sound of rapids—a rush of wind and water inside her head that, when it came, blocked out everything around her. It didn't happen often, but when it did, it was frightening, and it was driving her crazy.

The blank moments, as she called them, even had a rhythm. First came that sound, then a cold sweat, then panic with no reason. Part of her feared it was the beginning of an emotional breakdown. And part of her feared it wasn't—that it was going to turn out to be a permanent souvenir of her resurrection.

She was twenty-six years old and living the life of a senior citizen with dementia, and tonight was living proof. Here she was, alone in her apartment on a Saturday night, eating ice cream and watching the news like some old maid. All she needed was a cat.

Frustrated with herself and the situation as it stood, she stabbed her spoon into the mound of mocha fudge and then scooped up another bite, letting it melt on her tongue while she upped the sound on the TV and watched Pat Sajak bantering with Vanna White. A few moments later, an announcer broke into "Wheel of Fortune" with a special bulletin.

"This just in. Police are on the scene of a kidnapping that occurred only hours ago at The Dakota. Molly Dane, the five-year-old daughter of one of Hollywood's blockbuster stars, Lyla Dane, was taken by force from the family apartment. At this time, they have yet to receive a ransom demand. The housekeeper was seriously injured during the abduction and is, at the present time, in surgery. Police are hoping to be able to talk to her once she regains consciousness. In the meantime, we are going now to a press conference with Lyla Dane."

Horrified, Nicole stilled as the cameras went live to where the actress was speaking before a bank of microphones.

"I thought I had problems," she muttered, instantly ashamed of herself and her attitude.

When the woman began to speak, Nicole leaned forward, absently resting the bowl of ice cream in her lap. The shock and terror in Lyla Dane's voice were physically painful to watch, but even though Nicole kept upping the volume, the sound continued to fade.

Just when she was beginning to think something was wrong with her set, the broadcast suddenly switched from the Dane press conference to what appeared to be footage of the kidnapping.

The clip began inside the apartment. When the front door suddenly flew back against the wall and four men rushed in, Nicole gasped. Horrified, she quickly realized that this must have been caught on the Danes' security camera inside.

As Nicole continued to watch, a small Asian woman, who she guessed was the housekeeper, rushed forward in an effort to keep them out. When one of the men hit her in the face with his gun, Nicole moaned. The violence was too reminiscent of what she'd lived through to ignore. Sick to her stomach, she fisted her hands against her belly, wishing it was over, but unable to tear her gaze away.

When the maid dropped to the carpet, the same man followed with a vicious kick to her midsection that lifted her off the floor.

"Oh, my God," Nicole said. When blood began to pool beneath the maid's head, she started to cry.

As the clip played on, the four men split up in different directions. The camera caught one running down a long marble hallway, then disappearing into a room. Moments later, he reappeared, carrying a little girl, who Nicole assumed was Molly Dane. The child was wearing a pair of red pants and a white turtleneck sweater, and her hair was partially blocking her abductor's face as he carried her down the hall. She was kicking and screaming in his arms, and when he slapped her, it elicited an agonized screech that brought the other three running. Nicole watched in horror as one of them ran up and put his hand over Molly's face. Seconds later, she went limp.

One moment they were in the foyer, then they were gone.

Nicole jumped to her feet, then staggered drunk enly. The bowl of ice cream that had been in her lap fell at her feet, splattering glass and melting ice cream everywhere.

The picture on the screen abruptly switched from the kidnapping to what Nicole assumed was a rerun of Lyla Dane's plea for her daughter's safe return, but she was too numb to really pay attention.

Before she could think what to do next, the doorbell rang. Startled by the unexpected sound, she shakily swiped at her tears and took a step forward. She didn't feel the glass shards piercing her feet until she took the second step. At that point, sharp pains shot through her foot. She gasped, then looked down in confusion. Her ice-cream-spattered legs looked as if she'd been running through mud, and she was standing in broken glass and melting mocha fudge, while a thin ribbon of blood seeped out from beneath her toes.

"Oh, no," she mumbled, then stifled a second moan of pain.

The doorbell rang again. She shivered, then clutched her head in confusion.

"Just a minute!" she yelled, trying to sidestep the rest of the debris as she limped to the door.

When she looked through the peephole, she didn't know whether to be relieved or regretful.

It was Dominic, and, as usual, she was a mess.

Dominic Tucci was a six-foot-three-inch, third-generation Italian American, and the first member of his family to have a job outside the food industry. He'd been a member of the NYPD for ten years, and a homicide detective for the last three. He loved his job—and his downstairs neighbor.

He'd been on the scene only minutes after she'd arrived in the E.R., and had prayed like he'd never prayed before for her to survive. She had, and with what he was determined to view as only temporary complications.

He knew she was struggling with depression, but he also knew that nothing was going to change his love for her. He would take her any way he could get her—warts and all.

And loving her was only one of the reasons why he was at her door tonight. The other was the large, thick-crust pizza he was carrying—one half pepperoni, the other half cheese. Just the way they liked it.

He shifted the pizza box to his other hand and rang the doorbell. Moments later, he heard what sounded like breaking glass. Well aware of her tendency to stagger upon standing, he quickly rang the doorbell again. Just as he was on the verge of ringing a third time, the door opened.

"Hey, Nikki, I thought—"

His gaze went from the strained expression on her face to something brown running down her legs and the blood beneath her feet.

"Oh, honey…what have you done?"

"It fell," she said.

She hadn't mentioned what had fallen, but he knew this wasn't the time to press for details. As the door slammed shut behind him, he set the pizza box on the hall table and scooped her up in his arms. He carried her into the kitchen, leaving droplets of blood behind them as they went. When he set her on the island in the middle of the room, then squatted down to look at the bottom of her foot, he cursed beneath his breath. She'd really done it this time.

"Oh, baby…there's glass in your foot. Do you have some tweezers?"

"Top drawer on the night… I mean top drawer on the right…in the bathroom," Nicole said. "Alcohol and those…uh…those sticky strips…are in the cabinet on the middle shelf."

Dominic ignored her momentary word confusion to steal a kiss.

"I'm so sorry you're hurt. Hang on a sec. I'll be right back," he said, and hurried from the room.

Nicole sighed. Either the man was a saint or a sucker for trouble, because that was all she seemed able to produce.

He came back with his hands full of first-aid supplies and a look of concern on his face.

"Are you in much pain?"

"Some. It actually burns more than it hurts."

Dominic dumped the stuff he'd been carrying onto the counter beside her, then reached for the tweezers.

"Now then, let's see about getting you all fixed up."

Nicole sniffled. She hated herself for being such a loser, and hated herself even more for whining. But she had to admit she was glad he'd shown up.

"How did it happen, honey? Did you get dizzy again?"

Nicole frowned. "I guess...but mostly it was because I wasn't paying attention. I'd been watching the news when they broke in with a bulletin about a kidnapping. Lyla Dane's little girl." She winced as Dominic pulled a sliver of glass from between her toes. "Ouch," she muttered, then sighed. "I should be ashamed. Compared to Lyla Dane, I have nothing to complain about."

Dominic paused, then glanced up. "Look at me!"

When she did, he continued. "I don't want to hear anything negative come out of your mouth again."

Nicole shifted her gaze, silently admiring the perfect arch of Dominic's brows, as well as the warm, caramel color of his eyes.

"Nikki..."

"What? What? I'm looking, I'm looking."

He grinned. "But you're not listening."

"It's all your fault," she said.

His grin slipped sideways. "Why is that?"

"If you weren't so pretty, I wouldn't be distracted."

He laughed out loud. "Talk like that is liable to get you laid."

"Promises, promises," she said, and then bit her bottom lip as he removed two more pieces of glass. A few minutes passed before he had removed all the slivers. After that, he grabbed a handful of wet paper towels and cleaned the ice cream from her feet and legs before swabbing the cuts with antiseptic.

"What do you think?" she asked.

"About your foot? I think you could use some stitches in a couple of places."

"No, not my foot," Nicole said. "About the kidnapping."

"Oh. Nasty business. Sometimes being famous isn't all it's cracked up to be."

"I guess," she said. "And you can forget the stitches. I've been to the doctor too many times as it is."

"You're the boss," he said, and began opening some gauze pads to bandage up her foot.

His tenderness didn't go unnoticed. As he bent to the task, Nicole reached out and combed her fingers through his hair. It was black and thick, and straight as string. She loved the feel of it against her palm.

"You're a good man," she said softly.

Dominic paused, then looked up. The new growth of baby fuzz on her head gave her an innocent, childlike look, but he knew there wasn't anything childish about her. Before the shooting, she had been a vibrant, sexy woman. That woman was still in there, healing along with the rest of her.

"Thank you, baby," he said softly.

Nicole smiled a little self-consciously.

Dominic started to say something else, then hesitated. Now was not the time to broach the subject of their relationship. It was all she could do to get through a day. She didn't have the mental fortitude to deal with anything else. Instead of talking about their future, he returned to tending to her foot.

Nicole watched silently as he finished the bandages. Once he was done, she started to get down, but he stopped her with a look.

"Stay there until I get the rest of the broken glass cleaned up," he said.

Nicole's shoulders slumped. "Oh…yes, I forgot. I'm sorry to be such a bother."

He frowned. "Hey, don't talk about my woman like that."

She rode the surge of delight his words brought.

"So, I'm still your woman?"

"You better believe it," Dominic said. "Now, don't move. I'm still on the job."

Nicole laughed as he headed into the living room with a broom, a wastebasket and a pan of warm water. From where she was sitting, she could still see the television. They were playing clips marking Lyla Dane's rise to fame.

She frowned. Poor woman. Poor little girl.

"Hey, Dominic."

"Yeah?"

"Have they identified any of the four men, yet?"

He dropped the last of the debris into the wastebasket, wiped up the sticky spots and started back into the kitchen.

"What four men, honey?"

She pointed toward the television. "You know… the ones who were on the security tape."

Dominic frowned. "There wasn't any security tape."

Nicole rubbed the fuzz on her head in frustration.

"I know I'm not the sharpest tack in the wall these days, but there's nothing wrong with my eyes. There was footage. They were showing it right before you arrived."

Dominic frowned. He was Homicide, not Crimes, but he was pretty sure about his facts.

"Honey, I'm almost positive there was no security footage."

Nicole pointed.

"Damn it, Dominic. I sat right there on the sofa and watched four men kick in the floor…. I mean… door to the apartment. A small Asian woman, who must have been the maid, ran toward them. I guess she was trying to close the door. One of the men hit her in the face with a handgun, and when she fell, he kicked her so hard in the stomach that it lifted her off the floor. Then the four men cut up…no. Crap." She hit the side of her leg with her fist in frustration. "Not cut. Not cut. They split up."

Dominic laid a hand on her knee. "Slow down, honey. You're going too fast."

She took a deep breath, then sighed. "Anyway…it showed one of them running down a hallway and into another room. He came out carrying the little girl. She was wearing red pants and a white turtle-neck sweater. She was kicking and screaming, and then he hit her. At that point, the other three came back. One of them put his hand over her face and she

went lump…. No, damn it…that's not the word."
Nicole took another slow breath, then started again.
"She went…uh, limp…then they ran out of the apart-
ment. After that, they switched back to a rerun of
Lyla Dane's press conference."

Dominic was staring at Nicole as if he'd never
seen her before. The detail in what she was saying
was oddly specific, but he couldn't believe that the
cops had all that info and he didn't know about it.

"Hang on a minute, honey. I'm going to make a
couple of calls."

"Um…Dom?"

"What, honey?"

"Is that pizza I smell?"

He grinned. "You know it is."

Nicole arched an eyebrow. "So…why don't you
bring it in here before you make your calls?"

"You got it, baby," he said, then retrieved the
pizza, which she dug in to with relish, before pulling
his cell phone out of his pocket.

"Don't bother waiting on me," he said, as she
started demolishing her first slice.

Nicole looked up. There was a tiny smear of
tomato sauce at the corner of her mouth.

"Okay," she said, and took another bite.

Dominic grinned as he wiped away the pizza sauce
with the tip of his finger, then stuck it in his mouth.

"Um, tasty."

She smiled.

It took him a minute to remember what he'd been
going to do.

"Right. Phone calls," he said.

"So go make them. Thanks to you, I'm fine."

Dominic was too distracted by the shape of her lower lip to do more than nod. He was already dialing the precinct as she downed her last bite and reached for another slice.

Detective Andy Sanders had spent the last four hours at the Dane apartment and was just getting back to the station. With four kids of his own, he was sick at heart over what had happened to the little girl, but he couldn't let his emotions get in the way of doing his job.

They'd set up a phone line at the apartment for the expected ransom call, and several officers were waiting on site with Lyla Dane and her family.

His partner, Tomas Garcia, was at the hospital with the maid's family, waiting to see if she survived the surgery. If so, they would be requesting permission to question her. So far, she was their only witness to what had happened.

With all that whirling in his head, when his cell phone rang, he was expecting it to be Garcia. When he saw Dominic Tucci's name instead, he frowned as he answered.

"Hey, Tucci, what's up?"

Dominic heard the frustration in his friend's voice and could only imagine how busy they were, but he needed to make sure of his facts before he spoke to Nikki again.

"I'm just checking on a couple of things regarding the Dane kidnapping," he said.

Sanders frowned. "Since when does Homicide

have anything to do with kidnapping? Oh. Shit. Did the maid die?"

"No, no, nothing like that. At least, I haven't heard anything about her."

"Then what's up?"

Dominic took a deep breath. There was no easy way to ask this and not appear to be interfering.

"I heard a rumor that you guys have a security tape showing four men and the kidnapping going down. Any truth to that?"

Sanders cursed softly. "Hell no. We couldn't be that lucky," he said, then picked up a pen and began doodling on a piece of paper. "So who's spreading that crap? Hollywood?"

"No, not Hollywood."

Sanders frowned. "Then who told you that?"

"The maid...is she Asian?" Dominic asked.

"Yeah," Sanders said. "So what?"

"Did she suffer a blow to the head and then a kick in the belly?"

Sanders dropped the pen and sat up. "Damn it, Tucci, what gives?"

Dominic persisted, even though he was unsure of what this meant to Nicole's state of mind.

"Was the little girl wearing red pants and a white turtleneck sweater?"

Sanders's voice turned into a low, husky growl. "No one fucking knows this except the family. I want to know where you came by this information and who you're getting it from, and I want to know now."

Dominic glanced over his shoulder, making sure that Nicole couldn't overhear him before he answered.

"I came by to check on my girlfriend…. She got shot in the head during a drugstore robbery and nearly died, remember?"

"Yeah, I remember you telling me about that. So…she's doing okay, right?"

"I'm not so sure," Dominic said.

"Come on, Tucci. You know I'm swamped. I'm sorry as hell about your girlfriend, but enough about her. Who told you that stuff about the kidnapping?"

"She did."

Sanders froze. "She who? Your girl?"

"Yeah."

"When did she tell you this?" Sanders asked.

"About fifteen minutes ago."

"Where is she now?"

"In her apartment."

"Are you with her?"

"Yeah, but—"

"Stay right there," Sanders said. "Garcia and I will be over within the hour."

"She doesn't have anything to do with the kidnapping," Dominic said. "She's still suffering from the gunshot wound to her head. Hell, half the time she can't tell the difference between her right foot and her left."

"I don't care if she can't spell her name anymore," Sanders snapped. "She knows about stuff we haven't released to the press, and I want to know how."

"Just don't come over here and scare her," Dominic warned. "She's been through too damned much as it is."

The line went dead in his ear.

"Great," Dominic muttered.

"Who's going to scare me?"

Dominic frowned. He hadn't known she was there, but apparently she had heard every bit of his last sentence.

"A couple of detectives working the Dane kidnapping are coming to talk to you."

Nicole frowned. "Me? Whatever for?"

"They want to hear about that security tape you said you saw."

Nicole's frown deepened. "What do you mean? I did see it…. On TV, just like everyone else."

Dominic reached for her, but she pulled back.

"Don't touch me. I need truth, not coddling."

"There was no security tape."

Nicole's heart started pounding. The rush of sound was back, pushing inside her head so fast that she could barely hear Dominic's voice.

"But I saw it—all of it—right there on the TV."

"I'm not saying you didn't see something. What I'm saying is, you didn't see it on TV."

The sound was so loud now that it was like a roar inside her brain.

"Stop it…stop it now," she mumbled, and put her hands over her ears.

"Stop what, baby?" Dominic asked.

"The noise…in my head. Make it stop," Nicole muttered, and then her eyes rolled back in her head.

Dominic caught her before she fell. He was shaking so hard all the way to her bedroom that he was afraid he would drop her. He laid her down on her bed, then ran to the bathroom to get a wet cloth.

He was wiping it across her forehead when she came to.

"Dominic?"

"I'm here, baby," he said softly.

"I fainted."

"Yeah, I know, but you're okay. You just got a little bit upset."

"I always get upset when someone thinks I'm lying."

Dominic frowned. "I never said you lied."

"Oh, yes... I remember. It was more along the lines of 'I think you're, uh...lazy.' No. Shit. *Crazy*, that's the word. You think I'm crazy, or at least you should. I certainly sound like a nut job. I can't even form a proper sentence."

Dominic's frown deepened. "Damn it, Nicole. I never said anything like *that*, either. I'm going to get you something cold to drink. The detectives will be here soon, and the last thing you want to be is hysterical."

"Why?" she muttered. "Don't you know that crazy women can be hysterical all they want?"

"I'm not listening to this," he said, then shoved the wet washcloth into her hands and walked out of her bedroom.

Nicole got up from the bed, put the washcloth back in the bathroom and then changed into a clean shirt. If she was going to have company, it might be best if she wasn't wearing the ice cream she'd been eating earlier.

By the time she got changed into a pair of sweat pants and a T-shirt, and headed for the living room sofa, Dominic met her with a bottle of wine and two wineglasses.

"You're not still taking pain meds, are you?"

"No," she said, and eased herself down on the cushions.

He sat down beside her. "Good. You might not need this, but I do," he said, and poured the wine into the glasses, then handed her one, while he took the other. "To us," he said.

Nicole hesitated. "Why do you do this?"

He frowned. "Do what?"

"Still put up with me."

Dominic sighed, then leaned forward, cupped the back of her neck and pulled her close enough to kiss. Her lips were soft and warm, and she smelled faintly of mocha chocolate ice cream. He groaned beneath his breath as he finally pulled away.

"Because I'll never get enough of that," he whispered.

Nicole's vision blurred as she clutched the stem of her wineglass.

"To us," she echoed.

The perfect clink of crystal marked the toast. Within the space of two sips, the doorbell rang.

Nicole jumped, sending the wine dangerously close to sloshing over the edge of the glass.

"Easy, they're just cops like me," Dominic said, as he steadied her glass, then went to the door.

Detectives Sanders and Garcia nodded when they saw him, but they weren't smiling. His stomach knotted.

"Detectives," he said, as they entered. He gestured

toward Nicole, who was still seated on the sofa. "This is my girlfriend, Nicole Masters. Nikki, Detective Sanders and Detective Garcia."

Both men were slightly taken aback by the dark circles under her eyes, as well as the lack of hair highlighting a fierce scar on her scalp. Then there was the matter of the fresh bandage on her foot. She looked like anything but an accomplice to a kidnapping.

"Detectives, excuse my lack of manners in not standing, but as you can see, I'm still an accident in progress. Please have a seat."

They sat; then Sanders spoke first.

"I'll get right to the point. We've been told you have some information regarding the kidnapping of Molly Dane."

"I was watching the broadcast of the kidnapping, and then I saw..." She paused, looked at Dominic, then started again. "I saw what appeared to be a tape of the kidnapping from inside the Dane apartment. I'm told I was mistaken."

Sanders nodded as Garcia took out a notebook.

"So, Miss Masters..."

"Please, call me Nicole."

"Nicole it is," Sanders said. "We'd like to ask you some questions about this...uh...what you saw. I understand you said you saw four men."

"Yes. They kicked in the floor...." Her cheeks reddened. "Crap. I think I mean door.... They kicked in the door to the apartment.... At least I think they kicked it. It flew back so suddenly. Then I saw the maid running toward them. One of the men hit her in the face with a handgun, then, after she fell, he kicked her in the stomach. She was bleeding badly when they all broke...no, uh...you know, they..." She looked to Dominic for help.

"Do you mean they split up, honey?"

She sighed, then nodded. "Yes, they split up. One of the men came out with the little girl. She was fighting him, so he hit her. Then the other men came back, and one of them put a hand over her face, and after that she didn't fight anymore. Then they left. End of story."

Garcia was silent as he wrote quickly, intent on getting down everything she said.

Sanders was frowning. They had one witness who could corroborate the four men theory, but it hadn't been released to the press. The maid was Asian, and had injuries to her head and her midsection, the details of which also had not been released.

"You say you saw what the little girl was wearing?"

"Um...yes, she had on red pants and a white turtleneck sweater."

"Mother of God," Garcia muttered, and made the sign of the cross.

Nicole stared at him for a few moments, and suddenly the room faded away and instead she saw an older woman standing in a hallway, crying. Then everything shifted again, and she was once more inside her apartment. Without understanding why, she pointed to his phone.

"Your mother has been trying to get in touch with you all day. You need to call her."

Dominic was too startled to hide his shock. Before he could speak, Sanders attacked.

"What's that supposed to be? A…demonstration of your psychic abilities?"

Nicole was near tears again, but she was determined that these men not see her cry. She fisted her hands in her lap and stared the detective down. Her voice was shaking, but her gaze was firm.

"I don't have…abilities. Most of what I once knew is lost somewhere inside my head. I can't explain what I saw. I'm sorry I saw it. It wasn't pleasant to watch. I just want my life back the way it used to be…before someone put a bullet in my head. I just want to be normal again."

Sanders frowned. Part of him felt sorry for her, but he was certain she was either part of the kidnapping or trying to run some kind of scam.

"Lady, just for the record, there was no security tape, and you should not know the things you've just told me…unless you had something to do with the crime."

Dominic stood up. "Listen, both of you! Nicole is not a criminal. She's a victim. I don't know how she knows what she just told you, but I can guarantee she's telling the truth. If she says she saw this, then she saw it…somehow."

"So you *are* claiming that you've become psychic?" Sanders asked.

Nicole wanted to scream. Instead, she took a deep breath and made herself stay calm. "I'm not claiming anything. I just know what I saw, not how I saw it."

"Have you ever 'seen' anything like this before?" Sanders asked.

"No," she said.

Sanders chose to ignore Dominic and rubbed his bald head in frustration.

"So. In this so-called tape you claim to have seen, by any chance did you get a good look at the men's faces?"

"Only two of them," Nicole said.

Sanders perked up. "Do you think you could identify them if you saw them again?"

"Yes, especially the one who had the girl."

"Would you come down to the precinct and work with a sketch artist?"

Nicole's hands instantly went to her head. The lack of hair was still embarrassing to her, and going out in public looking this way seemed daunting.

"I, uh…I don't have any hair."

The tremble in her voice finally got to Sanders. He wasn't a woman, but he could imagine how devastating something like this could be to one.

"I don't either, ma'am, but it hasn't stopped me yet."

Nicole almost smiled. "Yes, well, I haven't been out since I came home from the hospital," she added.

"I'll get her there," Dominic said.

"But, Dom, my hair…" she said, and self-consciously rubbed her hand across the top of her head.

Sanders had the grace to look away.

"You're beautiful any way you look," Dominic said, then added, "I'll stay with you, honey. It will be okay."

She nodded. It seemed stupid to worry about going out in public with no hair when a child's life was in danger.

"Okay, I'll do it—if you'll do me a favor first."

Dominic touched the side of her face. "Anything."

"I need a hat…or a scarf…. Something I can wear over my head."

"Done," Dominic said.

Nicole nodded, then glanced up. As she did, she began to lose focus on Detective Garcia's face, then on her surroundings.

"No, no, not again," she mumbled, and put her head between her knees to keep from passing out.

Dominic reached for her as the other two men stood abruptly. She was moaning beneath her breath when Dominic put his hand on the middle of her back.

The moment he touched her, she sat up. Her eyes were wide open, but without focus, and she seemed to be staring at a spot above Garcia's head.

"There aren't any windows and she's afraid of the dark. She's been crying for so long that her eyes are almost swollen shut. There's a bruise on her cheek. A door is opening. Someone's coming. She's afraid— so afraid. She crawls up onto the bed to get away from the man who's coming in. She can see his silhouette and the red shirt he's wearing. It's got words on it. Minsky's Gym. It says Minsky's Gym."

Nicole shuddered, then blinked.

Sanders didn't know whether to believe her or not, but it was definitely weird. He looked at his partner.

"Did you get all that?"

Garcia was still writing when his cell phone rang. He glanced at Caller ID.

"Excuse me," he said, and walked into the kitchen. A few moments later he came back, pale and shaken. He stared at Nicole, and then turned to his partner. "That was my wife. She said my mother has been trying to reach me all day, but she got the numbers mixed up. She said my father has been in an accident and they need me to come to Boston."

Sanders wouldn't look at Dominic and couldn't bring himself to look at Nicole.

"Get going, then," he said to his partner, then looked at Dominic at last. "We're done here for now, anyway," he said.

"I'll bring her by in the morning," Dominic promised, as he walked the two detectives to the door.

Sanders made himself turn and look at Nicole Masters. She was sitting quietly, watching their every move. He glanced once at the baby fuzz just coming through her scalp and wondered what she'd been like before she'd been shot, then shook off the thought.

"Thank you for your time," he said. "We'll be in touch."

As soon as they were gone, Nicole began to breathe easier. "I think that went well, don't you?"

Her sarcasm was obvious. Dominic shrugged.

"They've got a lot on their plates, and it's hard for them to understand what's happening to you."

"I don't understand what's happening to me, either. I think I'm losing my mind."

He walked back to the sofa, pulled her to her feet, then lowered his head.

Their lips met.

The kiss proceeded.

Slowly.

Thoroughly.

"I think you're beautiful and you're exhausted, and that you need to rest, that's what I think," he said, and then picked her up and carried her to her bed. He stepped back after he tucked her in. "I'll check on you later, honey. For now, just sleep."

As the sound of Dominic's footsteps receded, Nicole closed her eyes. She heard the front door open, then close, and shut her eyes.

Chapter 2

After everything that had happened, sleeping was impossible.

Nicole spent most of the night on the sofa, staring at the ceiling. Every time she closed her eyes, she saw one disjointed image after another—of faces she'd never seen before and people she didn't know. It was as if seeing what had happened to Molly Dane had opened a floodgate. She still didn't know what to call what was happening to her, but she was firmly convinced that it had to do with her head injury.

Either she was going crazy, or she had been given some kind of "sight" into people's lives. In which case, even if she wasn't crazy yet, this could send her over the edge.

As time moved toward daybreak, she knew when

Dominic got up to go to work, because she could hear him walking around on the floor above. Just thinking about him made her weak with longing. They'd just been getting serious when she'd been shot. After that, he'd been the perfect boyfriend. Solicitous, sympathetic—always ready to help with whatever she needed. But there was a part of her that feared he'd stayed around only because it was the proper thing to do. She couldn't imagine a single, good-looking man willing to wait it out to see if she quit dribbling her food and falling over.

When she heard him getting out of the shower, she gave him a call. If she was going to have to go down to the precinct today, she needed to know details.

The phone rang twice before he picked up, and when he did, she could hear him chewing.

"What's for breakfast?" she asked.

"If I was down there instead of up here, it would be you."

She smiled. Their sex life had pretty much come to a halt after she'd been shot, but at least he still thought about it. That in itself was encouraging.

"Sounds interesting," she said, then shifted the subject before he felt obligated to make good on his threats. "Are we still on for the police sketch artist?"

"Absolutely," he said. "Just let me get to work and see what's happening before I block out some time."

"I can always take a cab," she said.

"I know, but I want to take you. I don't want you going through any of this alone."

Nicole was silent for a few moments, but there was something she had to know.

"Dominic, do you think I'm crazy?"

"Lord, no, baby…but I'm crazy about you. Does that count?"

"Dom, I'm serious."

She heard him sigh.

"I know, Nikki. I just don't know what to tell you."

Her voice shook. She hated showing weakness, but there was nothing she could do to change what was.

"But what do you think…really?"

His hesitation was brief, but his answer was firm. She could tell he'd been giving it some thought.

"I think something is happening that's scary to you. But if your injury has triggered some kind of psychic ability, I would look on it as a blessing, not something to fear."

"That's because it's not happening to you," she muttered.

"If it hurts you, it hurts me, too."

She sighed. "Okay, I get it. So I should wait for your call, right?"

"Right."

She disconnected, thought about trying to sleep, then changed her mind and got up. She had showered and dressed, and was downing some toast and jelly, when her doorbell rang. Surprised, she wiped her mouth, then slid off the kitchen bar stool and steadied herself before hobbling to the door. After a quick glance through the peephole, she let in the unexpected visitor.

"Detective Sanders, I thought I was supposed to go down to the precinct. Was I wrong?"

Sanders fidgeted without looking her directly in the face. "No, no. That's still on. I wanted to come by and show you something first."

"Oh, sure. Please, come in. How's your partner?"

He hesitated, then answered. "He's on his way to Boston."

"I hope his father will be all right," Nicole said.

Sanders eyed her curiously. She had yet to push it in his face that she'd predicted the call.

"Yeah, me too."

"Have a seat," she said.

Instead of sitting, Sanders reached in his pocket and pulled out a stuffed toy—a green Beanie Baby dinosaur—and thrust it into Nicole's hands.

The moment she touched it, she staggered. She didn't feel Sanders steady her or see the concern on his face. All she could see was a fleeting image of a three-story brownstone, then Molly Dane, standing in front of a mirror. As the child's focus shifted, so did Nicole's view of her location.

The room was no longer in darkness. What she could see of the furniture in the room was old and shabby. The floor was hardwood and in need of refinishing, and there was a blue-and-green spread on the bed. Then, between one breath and the next, the vision was gone.

She shuddered, then looked down at the stuffed toy and handed it back to Sanders.

"What just happened?" he asked.

"I saw her standing in front of a mirror. They're holding her inside a three-story brownstone, but I didn't see an address. All I do know is that she doesn't have any new bruises. They haven't hurt her again." Then she told him what the room looked like inside.

Sanders made notes as she talked, including the description of the room in which she said Molly Dane was being kept, then put the toy back in his pocket. He still didn't know what to think, but he did believe that Nicole Masters was serious. She believed she was seeing something, even if it was nothing but her imagination. Unfortunately, fantasy wasn't going to help them find the little girl.

"Well, it was worth a try," he said. "I may not be at the precinct when you arrive, but you won't need me. Frankie McAnally, the police sketch artist, is good at what he does. Hopefully we'll get something from the rendering."

"I'll do my best," Nicole said.

Sanders paused, then put a hand on her shoulder. "I know you will, and that's all anyone can do."

Nicole shuddered as a rush of wind blew through her mind, then looked straight into Andy Sanders's eyes.

"It's benign."

Sanders grunted as if he'd been punched. There was a knot in his gut that was making him suddenly sick, and his voice shook as he asked, "What did you just say?"

Nicole blinked slowly, as if she'd just awakened from a long sleep.

"The biopsy they did on your wife's breast…it's benign."

The color faded from Sanders's face. He turned on his heel and let himself out of the apartment without looking at her again. The minute he got down to his car, he called his wife. When she answered, she was crying. His heart sank.

"Nora?"

"I was just about to call you," she said. "The doctor just called. Oh, honey…it's benign. It's benign."

Tears blurred his vision. All he could think was that she'd been right. Damn it all to hell, she'd been right.

It was just after eleven-thirty when Dominic arrived carrying a yellow box with a large white bow. Nicole was finishing a tuna salad sandwich, and when she let him in, he blew her a kiss, then pointed to the tuna salad that was left in the bowl.

"Are you eating that?" he asked.

She grinned. "It's yours. There's thread in the thread box." Then she rolled her eyes. "Crap. Bread. Thread. You know what I mean." She pointed at the package. "Is that for me?"

He nodded as he spooned the tuna salad onto a slice of bread, then topped it with a second slice.

"Umm, good. Did you make this yourself?"

"Yep," Nicole said. "And nothing got mixed up this time."

He laughed, remembering when she'd salted her cereal instead of sugaring it. He gave her a wink and then took a big bite. As long as she could laugh at her situation, they were fine.

Nicole tore the ribbon from the box, then lifted the lid and pushed the layers of yellow tissue paper aside. She saw a flash of red, and then sighed.

"Oh, Dom," she whispered, as she pulled out a red crocheted hat made of the softest cashmere. It had a small ruffled brim and a perky little pompon on the crown. "It's perfect."

Gently, he cupped her head with his hand, dodging the scars and feeling the soft fuzz of regrowth.

"Is it soft enough? I didn't want anything that would be uncomfortable for you."

Nicole quickly pulled it down on her head, then hobbled to the mirror over the sofa. The fact that it made her look even younger was immaterial. Because what it also did was make her feel almost normal again.

"I love it," she said. "And yes, it's soft enough."

Dominic downed the last of the sandwich, helped himself to a can of Coke and drank it quickly. He'd promised to have her at the precinct by one. Traffic was worse than usual today, so they didn't have much time.

"Can you leave now?" he asked.

She nodded. "Just let me put on some lipstick and change my shoes."

He looked down at the bandaged foot and frowned.

"Can you get a shoe over that?"

"I have a pair of Indians…" She laughed. "I mean moccasins, that I wear as slippers. I'll wear those."

"It's pretty cold outside."

"I'll wear socks, too," she said, and walked carefully out of the room, still wearing the flirty little hat.

When she came back, Dominic realized that she'd changed in honor of her hat. She was wearing black slacks, and a red-and-black sweater. The little hat on her head was like the cherry on a hot fudge sundae.

"Looking good, woman," he said softly, then wrapped his arms around her and kissed her until her cheeks were as red as her hat.

"When we're through at the station, if you're not too tired, how would you feel about having an early dinner with me?"

Nicole's instincts for survival kicked in again. She touched her head, felt the red hat and sighed. She couldn't hide inside forever.

"If you're not ashamed to be seen with me, then I think I can manage."

Dominic frowned. "Don't, Nikki. You're alive. When are you going to realize that's all that freaking matters to me?"

"Then, okay, I would love to. My coat and purse are in the living room. I'm ready when you are."

A few minutes later, they were on their way downtown.

It was almost 5:00 p.m. when the sketch artist leaned back in his chair. Nicole breathed a slow sigh of relief. They had spent hours recreating the faces of two of the men she'd "seen" kidnap Molly Dane.

"What do you think?" McAnally asked, showing her the sketch of the second man. "Is the nose better now, or do you still want it a bit wider at the nostrils?"

Nicole stared at the face, then shivered. "It's him."

McAnally nodded. "I'll print these out and give them to Detective Sanders. He'll run them through the system. Maybe we'll get lucky."

Nicole's head was pounding, and she felt sick to

her stomach as she watched him walk away. She reached for the can of Coke they'd given her hours earlier, then realized it was empty.

"Here you go, baby. This one is good and cold."

Nicole looked up to see Dominic pop the top of a fresh can, then hand it to her. The slight fizz and the condensation on the outside were a promise of what was inside. She took a small sip, then swallowed slowly, savoring the cold liquid and the slight bite as it went down.

"Umm, good. Thank you so much," she said, then dug in her purse for some of the painkillers she hadn't needed recently but definitely required today.

Dominic had seen the pain in her eyes and knew she was exhausted. He pulled up a chair beside her, then sat down.

"Are you all right?"

Nicole nodded. "Just a little headache."

"You did great," he said.

She sighed. "I hope it helps."

He slid a hand along her shoulder to the back of her neck, then rubbed gently, massaging the knot he felt beneath his fingers.

"Do you want to go home?"

She frowned. "You promised me dinner, remember?"

He smiled. "I remember. Do you like Italian?"

She grinned. "I love Italians."

He laughed out loud. "You *are* getting better."

The sketch artist came back into the room. "Detective Sanders said to thank you for your help and that he'd be in touch."

"Does that mean I'm dismissed?" Nicole asked.

"You got it," Dominic said. "Do you want to freshen up before we leave?"

"Please."

After a quick trip to the bathroom, she came out to find Dominic in deep discussion with one of the detectives.

"Is something wrong?" she asked.

"No. Quite the contrary. One of the guys thinks the man from the first sketch looks a little like a perp named Raul Gomez. He's checking some details right now. In the meantime, we're going to dinner. I hope you're hungry."

"I'm starved," she said, and was surprised to realize she meant it.

A half hour later, Dominic pulled up in front of a busy Italian restaurant. A parking valet headed toward them, then opened the door for Nicole.

"You're going to love the food here," Dominic said, as he pocketed the claim ticket the valet gave him. Just before he opened the restaurant door, he bent down and kissed the side of her cheek.

"Hey," she said.

"Couldn't resist. It's that hat. You look like a pixie."

She grinned. "Pixie, huh? Just so you know, I'm too hungry to eat like one."

Dominic eyed the dark circles under her eyes and made a mental note not to linger over their food. She looked like she needed to be in bed, but he wasn't going to put a damper on her first journey back into normalcy.

"That's good to hear. My Uncle Dom owns the place, and he loves a healthy appetite. Since I was named for him, I'm his favorite nephew."

Nicole's hand automatically went to her head. The little red hat was firmly in place. Still, of all times to meet part of Dominic's family, she had to look like this.

Dominic read her mind. "They already know what happened to you. Like me, they're just grateful that you survived. Besides, I've been getting flak for not bringing you around before."

"Then why didn't you?" she asked.

He cupped her cheek, gently rubbing his thumb along her chin.

"Timing messed that up," he said. "If you hadn't been shot, this would have already happened. Then, afterward, I didn't want to scare you off until I was sure that I'd swept you firmly back off your feet."

"You lie," she said softly, "but that's okay. You just wanted to make sure I wasn't still drooling."

His eyes narrowed almost angrily. "No. I wasn't sure you could handle the truth, but since you've challenged me, lady, then you're going to have to hear the rest of it. I'm in love with you, Nicole. I've known it for a while. I just wanted to make sure that you remembered me…us. I didn't want to push you into something you weren't ready for."

Her jaw dropped; then her eyes filled with tears.

"Oh, Dom. You love me?"

"That's what I just said. No response is necessary. Can we go eat now?"

Too distracted to do more than nod, she let herself be led inside.

The scent of freshly baking bread and mouth-watering tomato sauces hit her like a lover's kiss.

"Umm, everything smells good," she said.

Dominic sighed. He'd said more than he'd meant to and was relieved that she hadn't balked. Maybe his uncle's chef could put her in a safer frame of mind.

"It tastes even better," he promised, then squeezed her elbow. "Hang on to that cute little hat, because here comes Uncle Dom."

Nicole barely had time to look up before they were engulfed.

"Dominic! Welcome, welcome. "

Nicole grinned. She'd never seen Dominic bow to another man's authority before, but his body language said he was definitely catering to his uncle.

Once his nephew had been welcomed properly, Uncle Dom turned his attention to Nicole.

"You must be our Nikki," he said, and then lifted her hand to his lips and kissed it in an old-world gesture that would have charmed her completely, had he not already done so by claiming her as their own. "Welcome. I hope you brought your appetite."

She smiled, then touched her head briefly, as if making sure the little red hat was still in place.

"I'm starving," she said. "Will that do?"

He smiled, then bent his head and kissed her on both cheeks before offering her his arm.

"Come, come…I will seat you at our best table."

Dominic followed along behind, smiling as they went. Nicole had fallen under his uncle's spell, which was good.

They were soon sipping a bottle of the house's

best wine while they decided what to eat. Nicole kept reading and rereading the menu, but the words had begun to run together. She was tired, and it was starting to show.

"Dom…"

"What, baby?"

"All the words are running together," she said. "Would you order for me?"

Dominic frowned. "I'm so sorry, Nikki. Are you sure you're up for this? We can always do it another time."

She nodded. "Yes, I'm sure. Order me something with marinara rather than Alfredo sauce. Maybe some eggplant Parmesan or shrimp prima vera. I love either one."

Dominic cupped the side of her face. "How about we order both and share?"

She beamed. "Perfect."

Dominic gave the waiter their order and was pouring some more wine in her glass when his uncle reappeared.

"For you, *bella* Nikki," he said, and slid a basket of warm bread sticks and some marinara sauce on the table. "Eat. Eat. You make me happy if you eat."

Nicole's smile widened. "That will make *me* happy, too. Thank you."

Dom's uncle winked at her. "You make Dominic bring you to Sunday dinner. You will meet all the family."

"Easy, Uncle Dom. I don't want to scare her off."

"Hey. I'm not that easy to scare, remember?" Nicole said.

Dominic's gaze slid from her shadowed eyes to the red hat and he tried not to think of how scared he'd been, sitting at her bedside in the hospital and waiting for her to wake up from the head wound—waiting to see if the woman he loved was still there.

"Yeah, you're a real tough one," he said, then nodded at his uncle. "Thanks again, Uncle Dom."

His uncle beamed, then moved away.

"He's really sweet," Nicole said, as she dipped a bread stick in marinara sauce, then took a big bite. "Mmm, so good."

The meal progressed and she found herself forgetting about her clumsiness and lack of hair. It wasn't until Dominic's cell phone rang that everything changed.

"Excuse me," he said. "I meant to turn off the ringer."

He was reaching into his pocket as she felt the noise in the room fade away.

"The maid died," she said.

Dominic froze. "What did you say?" he asked.

The phone rang again, but Nicole already knew what the message would be.

"Lyla Dane's housekeeper…she died."

A muscle jerked near the corner of Dominic's jaw. It was the only sign of what he was feeling. He looked down at the Caller ID, frowned, then answered.

"Tucci."

It was his lieutenant. "I know this is your night off, but considering the day you spent with your girl-friend, I thought you would want to know that the

Danes' maid died. Or…maybe you already knew it, since she's psychic and all."

"As a matter of fact, she mentioned it," Dominic snapped, furious at the sarcasm in his boss's voice.

There was a long moment of silence; then the lieutenant cleared his throat and continued as if Dominic hadn't spoken. "This has ramped up the pressure big-time. Now we've got a homicide to go with the kidnapping, and the mayor is breathing down our throats."

"Who's got the case?" Dominic asked.

"Miller and Betts. So if your so-called psychic comes up with another vision or two, you might want to share the news."

Dominic took a deep breath to keep from saying something he would regret later.

"If Nicole keys in on anything else, we'll be sure to let you know."

Dominic disconnected, then dropped the phone back in his pocket.

Nicole was watching him, waiting for him to look at her. When he did, she knew she'd been right.

"God," she muttered, and rubbed her hands over her face. "Why is this happening?"

Dominic glanced down at their plates. "Do you want dessert?"

Her chin trembled. "I just want to go home, please."

He dropped a handful of bills onto the table and stood abruptly. He waved at his uncle from across the room, then motioned that they had to leave. Before anyone could stop them, he had Nicole out the door.

The valet brought up the car, and they were soon driving away.

Nicole shivered. "I'm sorry for ruining the mood."

Dominic glanced at her briefly, then gave her knee a squeeze. "Honey, you haven't ruined a thing. We had a great meal and a good time, and now we're going home. The end."

She sighed, then leaned back and closed her eyes. Before long they were back at their apartment building. Dominic parked in the garage across the street, then helped her out of the car.

She stumbled.

He cursed softly, then picked her up and carried her across the street. Once inside, he put her down. They rode the elevator up to Nicole's apartment. When they reached the door, he followed her inside.

They paused in the foyer, staring intently into each other's eyes.

Nicole sighed, then took off her coat and hat, and hung them on the hall tree.

He waited. The tension between them was growing.

She looked up. "Dominic... I—"

"I want to make love with you."

She flinched. Without thinking, her hands went to her head.

"I'm not in love with your hair."

He sounded angry.

Her vision blurred.

"If you're too tired," he said, "then I—"

Nicole put her fingers on his lips, silencing the rest of what he'd been about to say.

"I want to make love with you, too," she whispered.

Dominic swallowed past the knot in his throat.

"Thank God," he muttered, and picked her up in his arms and carried her into her bedroom.

Lit by the faint glow coming from the living room lamps, they undressed in silence.

He finished first, then turned to help her. She had her shoes and slacks off, and was trying to pull her sweater over her head, when he took over. Within seconds, she was naked and flat on her back in the bed.

"Oh, Dom… I didn't think this would ever happen again."

Dominic hated the fear in her voice. He stretched out beside her, then took her in his arms. His voice was rough and shaky.

"Back when you were in the hospital, there were a few days when I didn't think it would, either."

Nicole swallowed a sob as she put her arms around his neck and pulled him down to her. His mouth settled on her lips for the slowest, sweetest kiss she'd ever had. His tenderness was unmistakable. She could tell he was afraid he would hurt her.

"I won't break," she said. "Just love me, Dom… like you used to."

He groaned.

The second kiss was overwhelming, sweeping through her last defenses as he took her in his arms. Heat spread through her body like a blast of hot wind. There had been so many days when she'd felt like she would have been better off dead. But this moment was a reminder of why she'd been wrong.

When Dominic levered himself above her, she

clutched his shoulders, urging him closer. Then he paused.

"What?" she asked.

His arms were shaking. He wanted her so much, but this was scary. "I'm so damned afraid I'll hurt you."

Nicole sighed. Everything that had been wrong with her now seemed inconsequential. Nothing mattered but him—and her.

"Only if you stop."

He gritted his teeth, then slid into her.

Nicole moaned. "Oh, Dom…so good, so good."

It was all he needed to hear.

And so the dance began.

Body to body,

Heart to heart.

They moved to the internal rhythm that only lovers can hear. For the first time since before she'd walked into that pharmacy, she was living again. Dominic gave her pleasure upon pleasure, rocking her senses until she was weak and breathless. At the point of being unbearable, it changed, breaking through her last defense and shattering her consciousness.

Dominic felt her climax and let go of the last of his control, following her up, then following her down. As she'd said…good, so good.

He groaned, then rolled, taking her with him until she was stretched out on top of his body.

"Are you okay?" he asked.

"Mmm."

He grinned as he tightened his hold. "So what you mean is…it was so good I've left you speechless."

She would have punched him, but there was no denying the truth.

"Mmm."

He laughed. Their world was back on track.

Chapter 3

The ransom call came at four in the morning, giving Lyla Dane until twelve noon to come up with twenty million dollars. At noon there would be a second call, at which time she would be given a numbered account where the money was to be transferred. They would have fifteen minutes to make the transfer or Molly Dane would die. Once the transfer was made, they would get a third call telling them where to find the child. Before anyone could object or ask to speak to Molly, the caller, wise to the presence of the authorities, disconnected.

Because the ransom call had taken so long to come in, Lyla had proactively offered a million-dollar reward for information leading to the arrest of the kidnappers. That had set off a barrage of tips that were driving the NYPD crazy. Despite the fact that most of the calls coming in were bogus, the cops couldn't ignore the possibility of a lead. And now the eight-hour deadline was looming. As for Nicole's sketches, most of the cops were convinced they were chasing ghosts.

But there was one lead that Detectives Sanders and Garcia—who was back from Boston, his father's injuries having turned out to be minor—were following up on. Early on, one of the homicide cops had mentioned that the first sketch resembled a man named Raul Gomez, a perp he'd arrested when he'd been working vice.

Hours before the ransom call had come in, they'd pulled Gomez's rap sheet, and made the rounds of his known hangouts and friends. According to the sheet, he went by the street name of Romeo and ran with an old cell mate from Attica named Ed Wolchek. Raul had fancied himself something of a boxer, and one of his hangouts had been Minsky's Gym. Sanders remembered Nicole saying that the man in her second vision had been wearing a T-shirt with the name Minsky's Gym on it. It could be a coincidence, but if so, it was an odd one, for sure.

The second sketch didn't fit Wolchek's description, but both Nicole and their one eyewitness had claimed four men were involved, so he could be one of the others.

The last known address they had on Gomez didn't turn up anything useful, other than the fact that he'd moved about a month ago and left no forwarding address, but they'd located his mother and were knocking on her door before daybreak.

Maria Gomez had come to the door in her robe and nightgown, taken one look at the badges that the detectives were flashing and burst into tears. They'd spent fifteen minutes calming her down and reassuring her that no one had died. Then they'd gotten down to business.

Maria Gomez was staring at the sketch in Detective Garcia's hand.

"*Sí, sí,* it looks like my son, Raul. Why do you have this? What has he done?"

Detective Sanders glanced at Garcia, then gave him a nod. They were betting on Maria opening up better to a man of her own culture.

Garcia leaned forward and set down a photo of Molly Dane. "You know this little girl?"

Maria frowned. "No…wait…is that the child of the movie star? The girl who was kidnapped?"

Garcia nodded. "Yes, ma'am. Her name is Molly. She's only five years old."

Maria clasped her hands to her cheeks. "Aiyee…the same age as my grandson, Manuel. Poor baby. Poor little girl." Then she must have made the connection between the pictures in her mind, because she asked suspiciously, "Why do you show me this picture?"

"The sketch we showed you, the one you identified as your son, is, according to an eyewitness, one of the kidnappers."

Maria Gomez sat up, then clasped her hands in her lap and shut down.

Sanders felt her withdrawal.

"I don't think that looks so much like my son after all."

Garcia shoved the little girl's picture closer, and the tone of his voice turned harsh.

"That baby is crying for her mama. Can you hear her? Strangers took her out of her room and into the cold. She's afraid of the dark. She wants to go home. Do you want that guilt on your conscience? What if that was your baby? What if it was Manuelito crying for his mama?"

Tears filled the old woman's eyes, but Sanders knew there was an unwritten law in her world that family loyalty trumped all. She didn't have it in her to give up her son.

"It doesn't matter whether it's Raul or it's not Raul. I don't know where he is. I haven't seen him in weeks."

Sanders frowned. That wasn't the information they'd gotten at his last address. According to neighbors, Gomez's mother had been a regular visitor to the place. He didn't figure Gomez as the kind to suddenly cut her off. Even the worst perps often maintained civil—even loving—relationships with family members. He figured Gomez for one of those.

"But you know how to contact him, don't you?"

Maria's chin jutted mutinously.

"Maybe I do. Maybe I don't."

Garcia picked up Molly Dane's picture. "If she dies and you did nothing to help, her blood will be on your hands."

Maria gasped and then crossed herself. "If I hear from my son, I will ask him about this thing."

Sanders sighed, then handed her his card.

"Time is running out for that little girl. Try hard… for Molly Dane, will you?"

They left without having accomplished much.

Two-plus hours gone. Five-plus left and counting. The pressure was on.

Nicole woke up to the sound of ringing. Thinking it was the alarm, she took a swing at it without opening her eyes. When the sound didn't stop, she rose up on one elbow, blinking in confusion. It took her a few seconds to realize she was hearing a phone. And that the phone wasn't hers but belonged to Dom. It took her another second to reconcile the sound of running water with the probability that he was in her bathroom, taking a shower.

With a muffled groan, she grabbed the phone and crawled out of bed. The cuts on the bottom of her foot were sore and healing slowly, which meant Dominic had probably been right about needing stitches. Still, she managed to hobble into the bathroom, carrying the ringing phone.

He heard the sound just as the shower curtain slid back behind him. Surprised, he turned around in time to grab the phone Nicole put in his hand.

"Alarm," she said, then frowned. "That didn't sound right."

He grinned as he turned off the shower. "It's a phone, baby, and thank you," he said.

She gave his wet, naked body an appreciative look as he grabbed a towel and exited the bathroom, leaving it all to her. By the time she came out,

Dominic was dressed and in the kitchen making coffee, if her nose was telling her the truth. She pulled on a pair of sweats and an old sweater, then stepped into some backless slippers and followed the scent of brewing coffee.

Dominic felt her presence before he saw her. Last night had been magic and he didn't want it to end. Unfortunately, the phone call had changed whatever plans he'd been thinking of making.

"There's news," he said, as he poured her some coffee.

"Good news?" she asked, as she added a dollop of cream.

"Depends on how you look at it," he said. "The ransom call finally came. They want twenty million transferred to a numbered account by noon today."

She frowned. "Transferred?"

"Yeah, it will make it a lot more difficult to catch them, and even after it's delivered, there's still no guarantee they'll give the girl back."

"Oh, Dom. I can't quit thinking about her. She's scared…so scared."

"I know, Nikki. We're doing all we can, but technology is making it easier for criminals to get away with things. However, Ms. Dane is also offering a reward of her own—a million dollars for information leading to the arrest and conviction of the people responsible. You might find yourself with a lapful of money, honey."

Nicole's frown deepened. "No way. I have all the money I'll ever need. I'll never need to work, though I love working part-time at the bookstore. Of course, that's over unless I can remember how to talk again without making a fool of myself."

Dominic brushed his finger down the side of her face. There was little to be said about her problems that hadn't already been said. Still, he could only imagine what she was going through.

Nikki leaned into his touch, but she was firm in her conviction about not wanting money.

"You don't understand," she said. "It took me years not to think of my parents' investments and life insurance as blood money. You couldn't make me take anything like that again. If these visions, or whatever you want to call them, keep happening, I don't intend to turn them into a damned business."

Dominic nodded. "I get it, baby, and I didn't mean to upset you. Consider the subject dropped."

She lifted her face for a good-morning kiss, which he gladly provided. Her senses quickened, but she let them settle. Dominic was already in work mode, and there was no time for messing around.

A couple of pieces of toast and jelly and two cups of coffee later, he was getting ready to leave. He was on his way out the door when she looked at him from the other side of the room.

"Call me," she said.

He paused, then turned around, took his cell phone out of his pocket and punched in some numbers. As soon as he finished, her phone began to ring. A bit surprised by the coincidence, she quickly answered.

"Hello."

"It's me."

She looked up. Dominic was grinning. For goodness sakes, he'd called her. She smiled back and asked, "What?"

"You told me to call," he said.

She laughed out loud, and he had to stifle the urge to close the door and take her back to bed.

"You're crazy…maybe crazier than me," she said, still smiling.

"I'm crazy all right…crazy about you, just like I said before. And just so you know, I lost something last night. You can be looking for it while I'm gone."

Her smile slipped. "Oh no. What was it?"

"My heart. It's here somewhere. When you find it, take really good care of it, because I've been trying to give it to you for weeks."

Nicole's eyes widened, then her voice softened. "Oh, Dom, that might be the sweetest thing anyone has ever said to me."

"I mean it, baby. You're everything I've ever wanted in a woman. I love you, Nicole."

She sighed. "I love you, too."

He nodded. "Then keep that thought. We have bigger things to talk about tonight, okay?"

Her heart thumped crazily. "Are you talking about the birds and the bees?"

He grinned. "We've already covered that subject. I'm talking about weddings."

She rolled her eyes, then ran her hand over the fuzz on her head. "That's what I said…almost."

"So…tonight?"

She swallowed past the lump in her throat, then nodded.

"Absolutely…tonight it is."

Moments later, he was gone.

At ten minutes to six in the morning, Raul Gomez's cell phone began to ring. He rolled off the sofa on which he'd been sleeping and reached for his phone. The only people who should be calling him were in the room. When he saw the Caller ID, he frowned.

"Hello, Mama. What's wrong? Are you ill?"

Maria Gomez was furious. She had a horrible feeling that everything the police had suggested was true. She loved her son, but not what he'd become. And there was the child. He had not been raised to be cruel like that.

"No, I am not ill. I am upset. The police were just here, looking for you. They think you had something to do with the kidnapping of that little girl who belongs to the actress. *Madre de Dios*, tell me you did not. Tell me that the sketch they have is not you."

"Sketch? What sketch?" he asked.

He hadn't denied being involved, she thought. His first comment had been about the sketch. Maria began to wail, claiming he was going to hell for his sins if the police didn't kill him first.

Raul groaned. Shit.

"Mama, Mama, stop crying. You don't know what you're saying. Of course I didn't do it. How could you think that of me?"

She screamed into the phone. "Shut up, Raul. If you can't tell the truth, don't talk to me at all. You never could lie to me, and you know it. You are lying now. I hear it in your voice."

Raul cursed. "Fine. Then I won't be surprising you if I hang up."

He disconnected, then, ignoring the three other men sleeping on various pieces of furniture, he turned on the television and flipped to CNN.

It would seem that things were definitely not going as planned. He would have sworn they hadn't been spotted, yet sketches of two suspects were being aired. Accurate sketches. One was clearly of him, and the other was Benny Jarvis.

The other three men woke up when the TV came on, and when Benny saw his own face on the screen, he leapt out of the recliner, cursing and waving his hands.

"Shit! Shit! How has this happened? No one saw us. You said so yourself. It's over. We're dead. We're dead."

Benny ran to the window. There were no cops lining the streets. He ran into the room where the kid was still sleeping, then back to Raul and the others.

"This is bogus. It's over. They know who we are. We gotta get out of here now!"

Raul grabbed his arm, then slapped him. Benny staggered, then fell onto the sofa with a thump.

"What did you do that for?" he mumbled, holding his jaw.

"You freaked. They don't know anything. Those are just sketches. They didn't give names. You didn't hear any names, did you?"

Benny shuddered, then shook his head.

"So calm the hell down. Everything is still fine. We just need to…readjust a few things."

"Like what?" Benny asked.

Before Wolchek had turned to a life of crime, he'd been a dockworker. He knew all about readjustments. Now he pushed between Benny and Raul, and took control of the conversation.

"The maid is dead. She can't identify us. The kid is next. We get the money, and we leave no witnesses."

Benny stared at the bald, muscle-bound psycho and freaked again. "No one was supposed to get hurt! You said so, Romeo, remember?" he said frantically, turning to Raul. "*Remember*? No one gets hurt. You said so."

Raul didn't comment. It was Wolchek who answered. "Shut the fuck up. Things change."

"I won't have any part of it," Benny said.

"I'll do her," Wolchek said.

Raul felt sick to his stomach. This felt wrong, but they were too far in to pull back.

"Fine," he said. "But not until the money is in the bank."

"No," Benny said. "I don't agree."

Raul leaned down until he was only inches away from Benny's face.

"You agree, or you die with her."

Benny paled, then dropped his head in his hands and began to weep.

Wolchek slapped the back of Benny's head.

"Suck it up."

Benny shuddered but wisely shut up. He knew them well enough to know they would make good on their threats.

Wolchek and Gomez turned to look at Jeff Whitson, who was Benny's cousin and the fourth man. He was also the computer geek. They couldn't kill him. They needed him to make sure the first transfer went as planned, then he would take it from there.

Jeff looked at the pair and then held up his hands in surrender.

"As long as I don't have to watch, do what you want."

Raul nodded. *"Bueno."*

They stood, watching the news anchor talking about Lyla Dane and her career, and when the broadcast flashed to a press conference that was just starting, Wolchek upped the volume.

The Danes' attorney was verifying that Lyla Dane was offering a million-dollar reward for information leading to the arrest and conviction of the people responsible for the crime. Suddenly Raul panicked. His mother was so pissed, he wouldn't put it past her to give him up for the money herself. And thanks to Wolchek, there was also a murder charge hanging over their heads.

Raul glanced at Wolchek. He knew the man had done a lot of bad things in his life, but volunteering to kill a kid was a new low. Still, five million dollars apiece was a lot of dough for four boys from the projects, and he believed their plan was solid.

As soon as Jeff could verify the transfer, they were heading to Canada in Wolchek's van. The ransom money would initially be sent to an account in the Cayman Islands. But they planned a twist on the game that the cops wouldn't be expecting. As soon as the first transfer was made, Jeff would transfer the funds again while they were en route to Canada. The second transfer would be to another account, this time in the Bahamas. And while the authorities were playing catch-up, the twenty mil would be transferred one last time, to a bank in Canada. They would have the money in hand and be gone before the cops ever realized what was happening.

Raul considered the plan genius, but they needed Jeff to make it happen. By this time tomorrow, they would be in Canada—twenty millions dollars to the good. The next few hours were crucial, though. He couldn't afford to have someone balk.

He glanced at the door on the other side of the room, listening for sounds to indicate that the kid was moving around, but he heard nothing. Despite his mother's panic, he was confident that everything was in place. She didn't know where he was, and the apartment belonged to Jeff Whitson, so even if she gave him up, they wouldn't know where to look. Still, just to be sure, he moved to the window, checking the street in front of the old brownstone.

The area was a beehive of illegal activities. The possibility of seeing NYPD black-and-whites was high at any time. He just needed to make sure they weren't here for them.

When he didn't see anything out of the ordinary, he walked away. This time tomorrow, they would be in Canada. The money would have hopped continents, and the apartment was paid up to the end of the month. When Jeff didn't pay next month, the landlord would just rent it out to someone else. No one would ever know they'd been here. They would dump the kid's body in the woods somewhere upstate on their way to the border.

What could go wrong?

All morning, Nicole had been aware of the clock. Knowing that everything was going down at noon was frightening. What if something went wrong? What if they didn't turn Molly Dane loose? She had tried, without success, to force another vision and finally given up, knowing that whatever was happening was out of her control.

It was just after eleven and she was in the kitchen, opening a can of soup for her lunch, when the air around her suddenly shimmered. The music playing on the stereo in the other room began to fade, and she felt the skin of her face tightening.

It was happening again.

She took a deep breath and leaned against the cabinet, waiting for the rush of wind.

It came, and with it came another vision. One moment she was pouring soup into a pan, and the next she was watching a short, stocky man walking toward her.

Thinking she was about to be attacked, it took her a few moments to realize that the man wasn't coming toward her. In fact, he wasn't even in her apartment. He was in the same room she'd seen before, and he was approaching Molly Dane. Somehow she was seeing through Molly's eyes—seeing everything Molly was seeing.

Then the man spoke.

"Here, kid…you gotta eat. I brought you a Happy Meal. It's got a toy in it and everything."

Nicole felt Molly's despair as the man shoved the food in her hands.

"Eat it!" he demanded.

In what Nicole could only call an out-of-body experience, she and Molly took the food to a table. She saw the little girl's hands trembling as she opened the small box and took out the plastic-wrapped toy. Without looking up, she set it aside.

Someone in the other room called out, "Benny, come here!"

Nicole saw Molly look up. The man, who Nicole now realized was one of the two men she'd seen at the kidnapping, glanced at Molly, then walked into the other room. As soon as he was gone, Molly ran to a window. It was boarded up, but she thrust her little fingers into a crack and pulled, trying to loosen the boards.

Nicole winced as she saw the child lose her grip. When she pulled back, her fingers came away with splinters. Molly grimaced with pain but had the foresight not to cry out. Instead, she clenched her fists, then glanced over her shoulder to make sure she was still alone before peeking through the crack. Nicole felt Molly's helplessness and despair.

Nicole's heart skipped a beat as Molly's gaze went from the graffiti-sprayed wall of the building across the way to the street signs at the corner.

"Oh, God…oh, God…look at them, baby. Look at the signs," Nicole whispered.

And Molly did. Her gaze went straight to the corner as if she'd heard Nicole's long-distance plea.

East 149th Street and Morris Avenue.

Nicole read the names twice, locking them firmly in her mind as Molly suddenly spun and headed for the table. She was tearing into the paper around her hamburger when Benny came back into the room. Benny was staring at Molly for what seemed like a very long time. Then suddenly he shook his head and looked away. At that point Nicole panicked. The thought ran through her mind that they weren't going to let Molly Dane go. Once the money was transferred, they were going to kill her. She had to tell Dominic and the detectives.

And just like that, the vision was gone. She glanced at the clock. It was less than an hour before the transfer had to be made. If they didn't find Molly before noon, it would be too late.

Andy Sanders and Tomas Garcia were on their way to the Dakota to wait for everything to go down. There would be the transfer, then a brief wait for the call that would give them a pickup location for the girl.

"What do you think?" Garcia asked, as Sanders stopped for a red light.

"I think we're screwed," Sanders muttered.

"We didn't get anything out of Gomez's mother."

Sanders shook his head. "No, and it's too late now to worry about it. Even if she knew something, she wasn't telling. "

"You'd think a million dollars would bring someone forward," Garcia said.

The light changed. Sanders accelerated through the intersection.

"We just didn't have enough time to make it work," he said.

His cell phone rang. He glanced at the Caller ID, then cursed beneath his breath. It was Nicole Masters.

"This better be good," he said, and answered the call. "Sanders."

"There's white and red and black gang graffiti on the wall of an abandoned building across the street from the three-story brownstone. From the window, Molly can read the street signs. East 149th Street and Morris Avenue. You have to hurry. When they get the money, they're going to kill her."

Sanders swerved, then tightened his grip on the steering wheel as he swung the car sharply to the curb.

"Say it again!" he yelled, as he put the cell on speaker.

Nicole repeated everything while Garcia wrote furiously.

"Hurry," she begged. "You have to find her before the transfer goes through or she's dead. Oh God… you have to believe me. Help her. She's so little and so scared."

"I hear you," he said, and disconnected. For a split second he and Garcia stared at each other.

"I know that area," Garcia said. "That's the Mott Haven section of the Bronx. I grew up there. What do you think we should do?"

Sanders shrugged. "What the hell. It's only my pension if she's wrong."

Garcia grabbed the radio and began calling it in as Sanders pulled out into traffic. He turned on the lights and siren, and stomped on the gas.

Dominic signed off on the report he'd just finished and was on his way to turn it in when his cell phone rang. He paused to dig it out of his pocket, then saw that the call was from Nicole and answered with a smile.

"Hey, baby."

Her voice was shaking, and it was all she could do not to scream. The urgency she was feeling was overwhelming. They all had to believe her. They had to understand.

"Dominic...I saw where she is. I saw the address. Molly was looking through a crack in the boarded-up window, and it was as if I was seeing through her eyes. She's at East 149th Street and Morris Avenue. It's a three-story brownstone that sits across the street from an abandoned building covered in white and red and black gang graffiti. I've already called Detective Sanders. I'm going to catch a cab and go there, too. If something happens, maybe I can still help."

Dominic flipped the report toward his lieutenant's in-basket and started toward the door.

"No, Nicole, no. There might be gunfire. You do not leave the apartment. Do you hear me?"

His answer was a dial tone.

As he sprinted for his car, the only thing going through his head was the call he'd gotten after the robbery, when Nicole had been caught in the line of fire.

"Please, not again," he prayed.

Chapter 4

Nicole wrote down the intersection that she'd seen in her vision, then grabbed her red hat, her coat and purse, and headed out of her apartment on the run— or as much of a run as she could manage with her sore foot. Her heart was pounding as she waited in the hall for the elevator. When the doors opened, she almost leapt into the car. As the car started to move, she automatically reached for her head, felt the soft red wool and thought of Dominic. There was so much riding on the vision she'd had. She wished he was with her. Maybe then she wouldn't feel so anxious.

When she got out to the curb to hail a cab, it dawned on her how cold it had become. She buttoned her coat all the way to the collar while wishing she'd brought her scarf. A single drop of rain fell on her face just as she realized she was only wearing one shoe. There was nothing on her injured foot but the bandages and a heavy sock.

Not only was she without a shoe, but she was also without an umbrella. She glanced at her watch, then discarded the notion of going back upstairs. In the grand scheme of what was about to happen, the possibility of getting drenched was definitely unimportant, so she turned her attention to hailing a cab.

The driver of the first empty cab to come down the street flew past without even noticing her. When she saw the second coming, she began waving and yelling as loudly as she could, but that driver, too, somehow missed her. When she saw the third one coming and realized it was empty, she jumped off the curb and ran into the street.

The driver hit the brakes, fishtailing slightly and leaving two streaks of rubber on the street as he came to a stop only inches from where she was standing. He was still cursing at the top of his lungs as she dived into the backseat.

"Drive!" she screamed and, not trusting herself to give the proper address, reached toward the bullet-proof partition between them and shoved the written address through the payment opening, so it fell onto the seat beside him. "There's the address. Take me there, and hurry. It's a matter of life and death."

The cabby was still angry as he glanced at the address. "Right, lady. I've heard that before."

Nicole leaned forward, stared at the back of his head for a minute and said, "You've been taking money from the church offering for the past six weeks instead of putting it in. Father Patrick knows you're doing it and is waiting for your confession."

The cabbie paled, his eyes widening in disbelief as he stared at her in the rearview mirror.

"How did you know that?"

"The same way I know that this ride is a matter of life and death. Now drive—and hurry!"

He took off, leaving a second set of marks on the street as Nicole grabbed for her seat belt.

She didn't know if it was going to matter whether she was at the scene or not, but instinct told her that the closer she was to what was happening, the better off they would all be.

Dominic was in a panic. He was running hot, with lights and sirens, and still afraid he wouldn't be in time. This thing that was happening with Nicole had him up against the wall. He didn't understand how she was doing it, but he was convinced it was real. And if he didn't get to her in time, it could very easily get her killed.

Suddenly he hit the brakes and swerved just in time to miss two black-and-whites flying through the intersection from the south. As he drove farther, it appeared they might all be going in the same direction, which meant Sanders had taken Nicole's warning seriously and put the word out. He had no way of proving it, but he knew in his gut that when they got there, they would find Molly Dane. Whether she was still alive or not would be their responsibility, not Nikki's.

Two minutes passed, then three, then five, and he was still at least five minutes away when he saw an ambulance turn off a side street and fall in behind him. He gripped the steering wheel a little tighter and stomped the accelerator harder.

The cab driver was performing what Nicole could only call miracles, getting through traffic, moving past construction areas by taking side streets and alleys, and all without giving her a backward glance. It was as if the immediacy of her panic had seeped into him, as well.

Nicole felt sick. She couldn't "see" anything else that was going on inside the brownstone, but she could feel it. Molly Dane's life force was dimming, as if the veil between life and death was thinner than it had been mere hours ago.

But she had hope. She'd seen a number of police cars going in the same direction they were. All she could think was, please, God, let them get there in time.

Suddenly the cab driver slammed on the brakes. Her seat belt popped loose, and she went flying forward, hitting the bullet-proof partition between them with her forehead.

"Oh, my God," she groaned, and clutched her head with both hands as the cab came to a stop. Another head wound? Could this get any worse?

"I'm sorry," the cabbie said, eyeing the swiftly rising lump and trickling blood on her forehead. "Are you all right?"

"What happened?" she asked, and wondered if it

was really beginning to rain in earnest, or if she was just seeing spots.

"See for yourself," he said, pointing forward.

She squinted past the pain, only to realize that the streets had been blocked, and that there were black-and-whites everywhere. They must be close.

"They've blocked off the streets, lady. I can't take you any farther. You want to go somewhere else?"

She scrambled for her purse, pulled out a handful of bills and thrust them through the pass-through.

"No. I have to be here. Thank you for the ride."

He pocketed the money, then frowned. "Are you sure? I don't think this neighborhood is what you're used to."

Nicole looked out the windows. "You're right. I'm not used to it, but it's definitely where I have to be."

She jumped out of the cab before he could argue, pulled her little red hat down tighter on her head and started walking. Almost immediately, she realized that the single shoe on her right foot was going to be of no use in keeping the sock and bandages dry on her left.

"I should have gone back for my other shoe," she muttered, then felt moisture on her forehead. To her horror, it wasn't rain, it was blood. There was a knot the size of an egg above her left eyebrow and blood on her hands.

Gritting her teeth against the pain, she started walking. She'd gone about a half block when it began to rain for real. She didn't look up, and she didn't look back. The farther she walked, the more certain she was that she was going in the right direction, because the sound of Molly's heartbeat was like thunder in her ears.

Her jaunty red hat was now soaked, and water was dripping down her neck. The bottom of the sock on her bandaged foot was stained a pale, watery red from the wounds that had come open, but she could see the police perimeter less than three blocks away. With her goal in sight, she lengthened her stride.

Then someone yelled at her.

"Hey, lady! You can't go down there!"

She paused to look behind her. A uniformed policeman was coming toward her at a fast clip. She couldn't stop. Not now. She started to run in an awkward, hopping gait that made her foot bleed harder. Cold rain peppered her face, but she kept going, terrified that if she didn't get there, it would be a disaster.

Suddenly the cop's hands were on her shoulders, yanking her to a stop. She immediately began struggling against his grip.

"Let me go! You don't understand. She's going to die if I don't get there in time!"

The cop, who clearly thought he had hold of a crazy woman, was pulling out handcuffs when a car came to a screeching halt in the street beside them. The cop was already reaching for his gun when he saw the driver fly out of the car, holding up his badge as he ran.

"She's with me!" Dominic yelled, as he raced toward her through the rain.

Nicole went limp. Dominic. She should have known he would come.

He swung her up into his arms and made a run for his car. In seconds he had her in the passenger seat and was headed for the driver's side.

The rain sounded louder from inside the car. Nicole began to shiver. The warm draft of air from the heater was blowing directly onto her feet. She sighed as the warmth began to seep in.

Dominic slid into the seat beside her, then frowned at the bleeding wound on her head and the obvious blood on her sock. The fact that she'd come out in this weather without proper clothing was crazy.

"Nikki...Nikki...what am I going to do with you?"

She grabbed his arm. "Take me down there, Dom. Please. Just get me there."

"Hang on," he said, and stomped the accelerator.

Nicole's panic began to recede. Dominic was here. It was going to be all right after all.

The rhythm of the windshield wipers was almost hypnotic. Dominic drove swiftly, passing a pair of black-and-whites parked at opposite alleys.

Nicole's hands were clenched in her lap as she looked up at the sky.

"Duck. It just had to rain. All we need now is for the rain to turn to snow."

Dominic began braking as he neared the perimeter; he parked near a pair of ambulances before he spoke.

"Duck? Why did you say *duck*?" he asked.

Nicole frowned, then rolled her eyes when she realized what she'd said. "That's not a curse word, is it?"

Dominic grinned. "Close."

She sighed. "It had all the earmarks of one until it came out of my mouth."

Dominic noticed her shivering, as well as the blue tinge to her lips. Without comment, he took the soaked hat from her head and laid it on the dash.

"My hat!" she said, and reached up to cover her head.

"...is wet," Dominic added. "You're wet clear through, your head is bleeding, and so is your damned foot." This his voice softened, as did the look in his eyes. "Nikki...baby...what am I going to do with you?" he asked again.

"Understand me," she said, and grabbed his hand. "I need you to understand me."

It didn't take a genius to figure out the answer.

"Consider it done," he said, and lifted her hand to his lips, kissing the white-edged knuckles, before rubbing them with his hands to get her warm.

Nicole peered through the windshield. They were parked at an angle to the brownstone. She couldn't see the front door, but, through the rain, she saw a boarded-up window on the third floor. The white, red and black gang graffiti on the opposite building confirmed for her that it was the same one she'd seen in her vision.

"She's in that room," she said. "The one with the boarded-up window."

His eyes widened; then he grabbed his cell phone and punched in a call.

"Sanders, it's Tucci. We're on scene. Nicole says the girl is in the third-floor room with the boarded-up window."

Detective Sanders was standing beside a SWAT van when he spun on his heel, quickly scanning the area for Tucci's car. When he saw the woman in the passenger seat beside him, he signaled the SWAT commander, who was about to send in a team. With a few quick words, they readjusted their plan of action.

Nicole held her breath. The building was surrounded by New York's finest, while more officers were going inside. She'd done all she could do. The rest was up to them. She just prayed the kidnappers hadn't done something irrevocable when they noticed the huge police presence on the street.

Benny came running into the apartment. He'd been loading their gear into Wolchek's van when he'd seen all the black-and-whites arriving. There was a brief moment when he'd seriously considered making a run for it on his own and leaving the others to fend for themselves. Then he thought of his cousin, Jeff, and bolted back up the stairs and into the apartment.

"There's cops out there! They found us! I told you we should've made a run for it. I told you. I told all of you."

Wolchek was the closest to the front door. He grabbed Benny and punched him in the mouth without saying a word. Before anyone else could react, he headed for the room where they'd been keeping the girl.

Raul was in shock. How had the cops found them? It must have been his mother. Maybe they'd traced her call. He couldn't believe she would give him up—not even for the million-dollar reward. Then he realized where Wolchek was going.

"Wolchek, leave her be. We've gotta get out of here. I know how to get out of the building without anyone seeing us."

"Not without the girl!" Wolchek yelled, and hit the door with the flat of his hand. It ricocheted against the inside wall with a thud.

Jeff was helping Benny up off the floor as Raul ran for Wolchek, who already had Molly Dane by the arm. She was begging and crying, and there was already a new red mark on her face where Wolchek had obviously struck her. At that moment, Raul had a revelation. He could hear his mother's voice, reminding him of how he'd been raised. He snapped and pulled a knife. The switchblade opened with a small but distinct click, revealing a long, thin blade.

"I said…leave her. She's not worth anything to us anymore, and we're not killing anyone else."

Wolchek took one look at the switchblade and slung Molly against the wall. She slammed into it hard, then fell to the floor.

Raul cursed. "You're a psycho, a damn psycho!"

Wolchek lunged, wrapping his hands around Raul's neck as Raul shoved the switchblade into his old cell-mate's belly. Then, for good measure, he pushed, shoving it upward, shoving it deeper.

Wolchek's eyes widened as his grip began to loosen.

"Damn you," he mumbled, then grabbed his belly as his knees gave way and he slumped lifelessly to the floor.

Raul moved past the body without giving it or Molly Dane a second look. Benny and Jeff were waiting for someone to make a decision, so he took control.

"Follow me," he said, running toward the kitchen.

The door to the old dumbwaiter was still there, even though it was no longer in operation. But it was a way into the basement. From there, Raul knew how to get into the sewer system without leaving the building. There was no guarantee they would get away, but they would have a better chance if the cops were occupied with rescuing the kid.

He wouldn't let himself dwell on the fortune they'd just lost, but it was clear that Molly Dane was of no use to them anymore, and there was sure as hell no point in killing her. If the cops already knew where to find them, that meant they knew who they were, which meant the kid being able to identify them no longer mattered.

As all hell was breaking loose inside, Dominic had Nicole sitting on a gurney in the back of an ambulance. A paramedic named Julio had applied a butterfly bandage to the cut on her head, then taken the wet sock off her foot and begun to swab the cuts with antiseptic.

"You needed stitches," he said, as he cleaned up the mess she'd made of her foot.

She refused to look at Dominic. "So I've been told."

Then, as he began to apply new gauze pads, the sounds around her began to fade. When she heard the sound of rushing wind, she knew it wasn't from the storm.

Suddenly she was inside the building with Molly again.

Molly was hurt.

Nicole could feel her pain, but she didn't know where it was coming from.

"She's been hurt again," she said. "It feels like her back...or maybe her shoulder."

Dominic had been watching the paramedic, but when he realized Nicole was swaying where she sat, he thought she was passing out. It took a few seconds for him to realize that she was "seeing" Molly Dane, instead. Then, when she began to speak, he jumped up beside her to make sure he got everything she was saying.

"Molly's watching them from the doorway. One of them is on the floor. The others are climbing into a small door in the wall. She wants to run, but she's afraid they'll see her. Oh! Wait! They're gone now. She's running for the door. Now she's out in the hallway. She doesn't know which way to go. She hears people coming up the stairs. She can hear their footsteps. She's afraid. She's afraid the men are coming back."

Dominic was on the phone, relaying everything Nicole was saying to Sanders, who had the SWAT commander with him, passing everything on to his men.

When the officers realized she was probably hearing their SWAT team coming up the stairs, and that the perps they were after were on the run, most likely heading for the basement, they rushed up the stairs.

Suddenly, through Molly's eyes, Nicole saw a team of armed men swarming through the door at the end of the hall. One of them was already calling out that they were the police. She felt Molly falter, then run toward them. Only after the first SWAT member had the girl in his arms did Nicole lose contact.

"She's safe," she said, and collapsed.

The minute the paramedic finished bandaging Nikki's foot, Dom quickly got her out of the way.

"They'll be coming out with the child any minute," he said, then carried Nicole back to the car.

The emergency personnel began to shuffle, preparing for the unexpected.

Police were swarming the basement. Within minutes, they found an opening into the sewers and a second SWAT team went in.

In the car, Dominic's phone began to ring.

It was Sanders. "They've got the girl. She's alert and asking for her mother. One of the perps was dead when we found him. We caught the others in the sewers."

"Good work," Dominic said. "Thanks for the call."

Sanders hesitated, then added in a lower tone of voice, "Yeah, well, tell your lady friend that we appreciate the help."

"I'll do that," Dominic said, and then dropped the phone in his pocket before turning to Nicole. "It's over, Nikki, and Sanders says thanks."

Nicole was weak with relief. "Thank you, God."

"Come on, baby...it's time you went home."

Nicole leaned against the seat and closed her eyes.

The rain stopped a few minutes before they reached the apartment. The sharp blast of wind cut through her wet clothes as Dominic helped her out of the car. By the time they got to the elevator, she was shivering again.

"God. You're going to be sick," Dominic said, as he pulled her close.

"No, I'm not," she said.

He didn't bother to argue. The proof would be in how she felt after he got her into a hot bath and then to bed.

Once inside the apartment, he put her bandaged foot into a plastic bag, then taped it around her leg before lowering her into a tub of hot water.

"Prop your foot on the side of the tub, Nikki. I'll be in the other room. Call me when you're through, and I'll help you get out."

She was too cold and tired to argue. With a sigh, she sank into the depths of the claw-foot tub and didn't stop until the water was at the edge of her earlobes. With no hair to get wet, she let herself relax.

"There's something to be said for bald heads after all," she muttered, as the water lapped at the back of her neck.

Dominic started the coffeepot, then went back to her bedroom. He stood in the doorway, staring blindly at her things, noting the slightly obsessive way she had of matching her clothes as they hung in the closet, and sorting shoes by color rather than by use. There was a pair of white tennis shoes sitting right next to a pair of white summer sandals and a pair of white fuzzy house shoes.

He looked at them for a few moments, then felt his knees give way. He dropped to the side of her bed with a thump and started to shake. Her phone call had scared him, but not as much as the sight of her on that street, standing in her own blood and struggling with a cop who was trying to handcuff her.

He swiped his hands across his face, then looked toward the bathroom door. The woman he loved more than life was behind it. She was still a little bit hurt and very fragile. This thing that had happened to her was unsettling, but he wasn't horrified by it as much as he was in awe. There was no doubt that she'd been on target with the kidnapping from day one. He didn't know if this gift would stay with her after she was healed, but he did know that it didn't change a thing. Not for him.

He reached into his pocket for the small velvet box he'd been carrying around all day. He'd meant to take her out to dinner tonight and make an occasion out of his proposal of marriage. But now, all he could do was be grateful she would be going to bed in one piece.

Minutes passed. He sat without moving, waiting for her to call. Finally her sweet but weary voice broke the silence.

"Dominic…honey…can you come help me out now?"

His hands were steady as he stood. The box with the engagement ring was hidden beneath her pillow.

He had her out, dressed and sitting on the edge of the bed within minutes. As she slid between the covers, then laid her head on the pillow, Dominic realized he was holding his breath.

Nicole looked up at him. Such a beautiful man. Shoulders so wide. Eyes so dark. Then she looked— really looked—into his eyes, and her heart skipped a beat.

He had a secret.

She sat back up.

"What do you know that I don't?" she asked.

She looked so young, with her hair gone and her face completely devoid of makeup. But there was passion in her. So much passion. He wanted it. He wanted *her*.

"You're not much of a psychic or you wouldn't be asking me that," he said.

"Dominic…don't play with—" Her eyes widened; then she rolled over and thrust her hand beneath the pillow. The look on her face was priceless when she pulled out the box.

To his credit, Dominic showed none of the shock he was feeling. God in heaven…she was the real deal.

"Oh, Dom…"

He took the box from her hand, then opened it and took out the ring.

"This was supposed to have happened over steak and champagne."

Nicole's vision blurred. "Oh, Dom."

He grinned. "You already said that."

She stifled a sob and held out her hand.

"Wait," he said. "I need to do this right."

He got down on his knees. "This isn't meant to appear as if I'm begging or anything, but I love you so much. I can't even see my life without you in it. Please…say that you'll marry me."

She swung her legs over the side of the bed and hugged him fiercely.

"Yes, yes, a thousand times, yes."

He slipped the ring onto her finger.

"Here's to forever," he said softly, then leaned forward and sealed the deal with a kiss.

Epilogue

One year later

Searchlights were sweeping the dark, choppy waters of the Hudson River as the Port Authority police cruised around the floating debris from the commuter jet that had crashed into the water less than an hour ago. With the plane completely submerged except for the tip of one wing and most of the tail portion, they were frantically scanning the surface for possible survivors. So far, the only bodies to come out of the Hudson had been lifeless.

A slim woman with dark, curly hair stood near the edge of one pier, staring blindly into the darkness. The man beside her was on the phone, repeating the short, staccato sentences coming out of the woman's mouth.

"She says there's a survivor. He's in the tail section of the plane and treading water. He tried twice to find his way out and nearly drowned both times. You have to hurry. Hypothermia is setting in."

Within seconds, they watched as men in wet suits went over the side of one of the search boats and slipped beneath the dark water.

Motionless, Nicole felt the trapped survivor's fear, but had no way to assure him that help was on the way, even though she was in his head, sharing the darkness with him. It wasn't until the man saw the divers' searchlights begin cutting through the water around him that she felt his relief and thanksgiving.

She went limp.

Dominic had been waiting for it. It was the sign that told him it was over. He slid an arm across her shoulders to remind her that he was there if she needed him. When she leaned against him, he gave her arm a squeeze.

"They found him. It's over," she said.

"Is it safe to go home now?"

She nodded. Concern was in Dom's voice—compassion in his eyes. But it was his confidence in her that mattered most.

"Yes. We can go home now."

He took her by the hand, and together they walked toward the car, moving past all the dozens of police and emergency vehicles.

As they got inside, Nicole reached for her seat belt, then paused, watching as her husband slid behind the wheel. His dark hair was windblown, his eyes red-rimmed, and he was as weary looking as she felt. But then their gazes met. When he winked and smiled, she smiled back.

"If you're a real good girl, I've got a surprise waiting for you at home."

Nicole laughed out loud. "I'm always good."

He grinned. "No. You're outstanding. However, I am not talking about sex."

"But I was."

"Good," Dominic said. "Then you won't be disappointed by the surprise."

She closed her eyes as he drove away from the scene. The farther away he drove, the lighter her heart became. Distancing herself from despair was part of the separation she needed to gain control of her own thoughts.

Her life was strange now, but as Dominic reminded her on a daily basis, it didn't matter. If they had to interrupt their lives now and then to help someone in danger, then so be it.

It was a quarter to three in the morning when they got back to the apartment. Dominic unlocked the door, then surprised Nicole by picking her up and carrying her inside.

She leaned her head against his chest as he carried her into the bedroom, then sat her down on the side of the bed.

"Ooh, it feels good to be home," she said, as she began to kick off her shoes.

When she looked up, Dominic was at the bureau. As he turned around, she saw something in his hand.

"What's that?" she asked, as he sat down beside her.

He was holding a long silver chain.

"Tomorrow is our anniversary, but I thought, considering everything that was going on…"

She held out her hand as he dropped the silver chain into her palm and she saw the charm on the necklace. When she realized what it was, her vision blurred.

"Oh, Dominic, it's perfect."

She looked up at him, smiling through tears.

He smiled, pleased that he'd actually surprised her.

"The way I figured it, every little witch needs a crystal ball."

"So I'm a witch, am I?"

"Yes. But you're my witch," he added.

Suddenly she stood up and began stripping off her clothes until she was standing naked before him. She gave him a slow, sultry glance, handed him the necklace, then turned her back.

"Would you please put it on me?"

Dominic's concentration had shattered when she'd begun taking off her clothes. Now she wanted him to maneuver something this delicate when his damn fingers all felt like thumbs?

The small silver-and-crystal charm was cold between her breasts as she turned around and pretended to stare into the tiny crystal ball.

"I foresee a long session of passionate sex," she said.

"Thanks for the warning. Now I know what to expect," he said, as he laid her in the bed, then began taking off his clothes.

Nicole rose up on her elbow to watch, the small crystal ball dangling between her breasts.

"You're wrong, my love," Nicole said softly. "You have no idea of what's coming."

Dominic laughed out loud as he fell into bed beside her, then in one swoop, covered her body with his own.

"That's okay, my little witch. I always did like surprises."

AFTER THE LIGHTNING

Janis Reams Hudson

Dear Reader,

Did you ever get stuck in a rut for so long that it became comfortable? You know, that same ol' route to work, while you nag about the bad road, when another road will take you there, a better road. It's just not your road, so you forget about it?

Or perhaps the same meals each successive week. My mother did that. Monday night was tacos. The only kind we had in town that year were the frozen kind. Hmm. Yum. Sunday was roast beef. That was good. Thankfully I've forgotten the rest. Not that they weren't good, but the same ones for each night of the week, over and over for ten years...

I'm not griping about my mother, though. She worked two jobs to put that food on the table.

Not all people have a good mother or an available alternate route. Some of us just have to stand and face the winds of life on our own and drive that same old route while we look for something better. Eat that taco Monday. But along the way, if life pushes you into the path of someone special, slow down. Reach out and offer a hand if they need help, or ask for help if *you* do.

In my story, lifelong bonds are formed when people stop to help each other—a girl struck by lightning, an investigator on the trail of a bad guy, plus a missing child whose mother is in a coma. Well, her body is. But since lightning has turned our heroine into a receptor of sorts, things get interesting.

Hope you enjoy my story. And if you do, please tell two friends.

Happy reading,

Janis Reams Hudson

Dedicated to

Sharon, for nursing me through this story

And Deb, the third sister in this deal

Chapter 1

One minute she was jogging along, two blocks from home, enjoying the outdoors, the sunshine, the strong wind. Then suddenly, every hair on her body stood on end and the air exploded around her. The smell of sulphur nearly knocked her over, and a giant fist struck her in the chest and lifted her off the ground.

After that, Hailey Cameron didn't know anything until she found herself lying flat on her back staring up at fluorescent lighting while two nurses and a doctor poked and prodded her. This time it was the smell of antiseptic that stung her eyes and nose.

"Honey, you must be the luckiest girl on earth."

"Wha...?" She tried to ask what had happened, where she was, how had she gotten here, why her skin was tingling, could she have a drink of water, *what day is it?* But her voice wouldn't work. Her fingers and toes seemed to move okay, but she couldn't decide if what she felt overall was a dull ache or numbness or out-and-out pain. She felt vaguely as if she'd been run over by a truck. Twice.

"You just rest now, and lie still," the nurse ordered. "You're in Baton Rouge Hospital. Can you tell me your name?"

"Why?" Hailey managed.

"You got struck by lightning."

"What?" Hailey struggled against the hands that held her down.

"Easy, now. Stop that. Can you tell me your name?" the nurse repeated.

"Hailey." She paused and licked her lips. "Hailey Cameron." She chose that moment to glance down. "Yikes! Why am I naked?"

"Relax, relax. Here." The nurse covered Hailey with a sheet. "That's better. We had to cut off what was left of your clothes to check you for injuries."

"Cut them?" Hailey's voice was coming back, and her brain was clearing rapidly. "You cut up my clothes? Am I supposed to go home naked?"

"You're not supposed to go home at all," the nurse announced. "Not until tomorrow. We don't get all that many lightning strike victims. The doctor wants to keep you overnight for observation. And no, we won't send you home naked. There wasn't enough left of your clothes, anyway. The lightning shredded them."

Hailey was so out of it that it took her a minute to

grasp everything that had happened, especially that the doctor and nurses meant for her to spend the night in the hospital. She tried to gather enough strength to protest but found she'd used all her energy already. The few words she'd managed had drained her. She gave up the effort and dozed.

They woke her sometime later to tell her to lie still for a CT scan of her brain.

Then there were the X rays, blood tests, ECG and heaven knew what else.

She woke again in the middle of being transferred from gurney to bed in a semiprivate room. Room 312, they told her. Was she supposed to care about the room number?

The nurses tried repeatedly to get her oxygen to work, but no matter what they did, nothing came from the connection in the wall above her bed. No stream of oxygen, not even a puff.

"Stupid thing," one nurse muttered. "Terry," she said to the orderly, "see if there's a concentrator in the supply closet down the hall. Not to worry." She smiled at Hailey. "We'll get you all fixed up in no time."

Hailey could still feel a slight tingle along her skin. It might have been pleasant, but it was lasting way too long. To take her mind off it, she glanced around the room. Plain white walls, one window with white miniblinds, a white curtain ready to pull between her bed and the next one.

"Who's that?" she asked, nodding toward the woman in the other bed. "What's wrong with her?"

"That's LaShonda Martin. Bless her heart, she

was in that apartment building that was hit by the tornado last night."

"Ouch," Hailey said in sympathy. "Sorry to hear about your troubles," she said, louder, so her roommate could hear her. "I'm Hailey."

"Talk all you want, *cher*." The nurse hung the IV from the bag holder beside Hailey's bed. "She can't answer. We've got her in a drug-induced coma until some of her injuries heal and she's over the worst of the pain. Ah, here we go."

The orderly wheeled in a machine that stood about as tall as Hailey's bed and was about eighteen inches wide. He and the nurse fiddled with filters that looked like thin sponges, a humidifier for distilled water and a clear hose that connected to the tube running into Hailey's nose.

"Oxygen?" she asked.

"Yes, ma'am. When we turn it on it will suck in air from the room. It will filter out all the nitrogen and impurities until all that's left for you to breathe is pure oxygen."

The nurse pushed the on switch, but nothing happened. She and the orderly fussed over the power cord.

Hailey swallowed and tuned out their voices. Her gaze trailed over to her roommate. If that tornado had touched down a mile sooner, that could be her in a coma in that bed by the window. "Is she in pain?"

"If she is," the nurse said, "she doesn't know it, so I guess she's not."

In the next bed, LaShonda Joy Martin tried to

scream in frustration, but all she managed was a pitiful whimper she knew no one could hear.

Something was wrong. A lot of things were wrong, the biggest being that her son was missing. How could she find him if she was trapped in this ever-lovin' coma? Yet, if she was in a coma, why could she hear and see everything around her? With her eyes closed. Why did she feel like she was floating in and out of her body, like gravity was letting go of her? If a good stiff wind blew through the room, she would be swept away from her body and right on out the door.

She wondered what they were talking about over there at the other bed. Could one of them find her baby boy?

She tried to raise her head, but it wobbled, then flopped down. *Come on, dammit.* She tried again with all her might, until finally she managed to sit up far enough that she could see the foot of her bed. She turned her head and saw the nurse, the orderly and her new roommate. And from the corner of her eye, she saw herself, lying on the bed.

Her heart leapt into her throat. How could she be lying down and sitting up at the same time? From her head to her toes, she started to shake. She shook hard enough to vibrate the bed. But the bed did not move. Not even the sheets moved.

From that odd machine the orderly had wheeled in a few minutes earlier came a long, loud beep. The air began to stir. The wind tugged on her. She grabbed the sheet to hold on, but when she closed her fist, there was no sheet in it. What was happening?

No matter how hard she tried to stay put, she was no match for the air current sweeping the room. She was being pulled inexplicably toward that noisy machine. But her body remained motionless on the bed.

A sudden swirl of air literally sucked her away. She screamed. No one heard her.

Like a heat-seeking missile, she shot headfirst into the air intake valve of the oxygen concentrator. She waited for the pain, waited to feel her flesh being peeled from her bones. But her body still lay on the bed behind her. She felt no pain at all. Only sheer terror as she was sucked through one filter after another, then up through a series of clear plastic tubes and…up her roommate's *nose*?

Oh, my God.

The voice echoed inside Hailey's head, sounding utterly miserable.

"How can she talk if she's in a coma?" Hailey asked.

"Who?" the nurse asked, distracted, as she straightened a tube.

"Her," Hailey said. "LaShonda."

The nurse double checked the IV in Hailey's hand. "She can't talk, remember? She's in a coma. She must have moaned."

Hailey eyed the nurse warily. "So how come I hear her voice?"

Slowly, the nurse asked, "You're hearing voices?"

"Only one. Hers, I think."

A tearful voice rang inside Hailey's head. *You think? You* think? *Who else's voice could it be but mine? I'm LaShonda Joy Martin. I'm right here in*

*your head, and I'm not going anywhere 'til you help
me find my baby.*

Hailey stared at the nurse. "You're telling me you
didn't hear that?"

"Hear what?"

"Oh, brother," Hailey muttered. "Am I losing my
mind?"

"I doubt it," the nurse said easily. "I'll talk to your
doctor, but it's probably just some temporary leftover
electrical mix-up in your brain from the lightning."

The nurse patted her on the arm, then left the
room, leaving Hailey alone. Sort of.

You gotta help me, the voice said.

"Says who? You're an electrical impulse in my
brain," Hailey said firmly. "I don't have to help an
electrical impulse."

I'm not any ol' impulse. I'm LaShonda Martin.

"LaShonda Martin is in a coma. I'm staring at her
right now."

*Yeah. Somebody oughta comb my hair for me.
Damn.* The latter came out in a deep-South two-
syllable way, as day-*yum.*

"Your lips aren't moving," Hailey accused. "If I
can hear your voice, why don't I see your lips
move?"

Because I'm in a coma.

"I rest my case," Hailey said. "If you're in a coma,
you can't be talking."

A loud sigh echoed in Hailey's brain. *Look. My
body is—*

A dark arm—too dark for a simple tan—pointed
toward LaShonda's bed, and Hailey screamed,

because both of her own arms—her own tanned but
definitely Caucasian arms—were still lying at her
sides.

*Day-yum, white girl, hold it down, will ya? You
nearly scared me to death.*

"Me? Scare you? I've suddenly sprouted a third
arm. What the hell is going on? How did you get
in my head?"

*Don't you yell at me. It isn't my fault I'm stuck in
here like a sardine in a can. I was just lying there
minding my own business, trying to stay in my body,
but I kept floating up and out, ya know?*

"No, I don't know. You mean you died?"

*No, I didn't die. Look at those machines, all
beeping just like they're supposed to. I'm alive. But
while my body's in a coma, I guess the rest of me
isn't. When they turned on your oxygen machine I got
sucked in, right through the filter and that skinny
little tube, and straight up your dainty white nose.
You ain't lived 'til you've been up inside somebody
else's nose, let me tell you. It's not something I ever
wanna do again, that's for sure.*

"Well, then, get out," Hailey demanded.

The voice was silent for several long moments.

"Hey." Hailey felt stupid and self-conscious
talking to someone who wasn't there. "LaShonda?
Did you leave?"

You told me to.

"Yes, but did you?"

There was a distinct sniff, then, *I don't know how.*

"What do you mean, you don't know how?"

I mean, I don't know how to leave, LaShonda

said, sounding very much as if she thought she was talking to an idiot.

"Why don't I blow my nose?" Hailey asked tersely. "Maybe you'll end up in my tissue."

Oooh, gross. LaShonda made a gagging noise.

Out in the hallway, Aaron Trent, a special investigator for the District Attorney, folded his arms and leaned against the wall, waiting for the woman in Room 312 to finish her phone conversation. From the sound of things, she and whomever she was talking to were not getting along.

After nearly ten minutes, he was getting antsy. Somebody was going to call security on him for loitering if he had to hang around out there much longer.

Finally he approached the open door and leaned in…only to find, to his surprise, that the woman he'd been listening to all this time was not on the phone. She couldn't even reach the phone from where she lay. She was talking to herself.

That fact took him so much by surprise that he must have made a sound, and he failed to duck back out of sight before she spotted him.

His brothers and sisters would give him holy hell for hanging around and waiting on a woman who spoke to herself. His grandmother would thoroughly enjoy the idea.

Not that he planned to tell any of them. He would never live it down. He took a deep breath, walked in and gripped the foot of the bedframe.

"Hi," he offered with a smile.

She frowned. "Don't tell me you're another doctor."

"Okay, I won't tell you." She looked a little ragged, but not nearly as ragged as he'd imagined someone recently struck by lightning might look.

"Who are you?" she asked.

"Aaron Trent. I'm a special investigator with the district attorney's office." He flashed his badge, then tucked it away. "You're Hailey Cameron, the woman who was struck by lightning this afternoon, right?"

"Unless there's someone else around here with singed hair and shredded clothes."

He narrowed his eyes with interest. *Shredded clothes? So does that mean you're—*

She stared right back at him. "Don't be ordinary, Mr. Trent."

Aaron straightened in surprise. He knew he hadn't spoken aloud. Had she read his mind? Regardless, he'd learned long ago from the women in his family that if a man was in doubt, the best course was to apologize. It didn't matter if he'd done anything wrong or not; he just needed to apologize. He gave Hailey a short bow. "My apologies."

Her gaze sharpened. "For what?"

"For being ordinary?"

"Nice save. What do you want with the woman who got hit by lightning?"

"I'm actually looking for the woman who lives in the white house on the corner of the street you were on when the lightning struck you. I understand you run the same route past that house nearly every day. Maybe you've seen her lately? She's elderly, stooped shoulders, white hair."

"You seem to know a lot about her…and me."

"That's my job, finding out information. Do you know the woman I'm talking about?"

"Mrs. Shelton?"

Aaron felt the tension between his shoulder blades ease. "So you know her."

"I do. I've missed her lately, though. Haven't seen her around. Is she all right?"

Damn. He'd been hoping… "I'd know more about that if I could find her. How well do you know her?"

"She likes to interrupt my jogging by standing on her porch with a glass of iced tea or lemonade for me, with enough sweat dripping off the glass to make me beg. Gets me every time. I can't imagine she's done something to warrant the D.A. sending out a special investigator."

"Ah, no. I just have a few questions for her. I'm trying to find her nephew. I was hoping she could help me."

She shrugged, then twitched, as if she'd been slapped, or maybe poked. "Maybe you could help a, uh, friend of mine. Help us find her little boy."

That was just about the last question he'd expected her to ask. He was no expert on finding missing children, but wasn't it the same as finding the bad guys who took them? He could find bad guys. He was good at that. He'd done it as a cop, and he was still doing it. He was after one right now.

"What happened to the kid?" Aaron asked Hailey.

She had a way of tilting her head before speaking, as if thinking over her words before opening her mouth. Or perhaps listening to some inner voice before she spoke. It was an odd habit, but her smile was so distracting that he might not have noticed the way her gaze turned inward if he weren't a trained observer. And if he didn't have Claudia Jean Trent for his grandmother.

"The tornado," Hailey said.

"The tornado took him? Somebody must have found him by now," Aaron stated. "When was he reported missing?"

"Not the tornado, *after* the tornado. He never got reported missing until now because I—" She stopped and swallowed. "Because his mother has been in a coma since they brought her to the hospital." She waved her arm toward the other bed.

"She's the boy's mother?"

"That's right. LaShonda Joy. Martin. LaShonda Joy Martin."

"She and the boy—"

"Keenan. Keenan Martin. Four years old. And beautiful." Emotion made her voice wobble.

"They lived in that apartment complex that got hit last night?"

"Yes. But they came through the tornado fine," she said in a rush. "There was plenty of damage to their unit, but they rode it out in the bathtub with a mattress on top of them." She paused again.

"And…?" he prodded.

"And…a man came and pulled the rubble off of them. He took Keenan and said he would get him out of there before anything else fell down on them, and then he'd come back for LaShonda. He was only going to the street, so she thought it was okay."

"Did the guy come back for her?"

"We assume he did."

"Assume?"

She nodded. "Someone beat the daylights out of her. I'm told it took the surgeons all night to put her face and skull back together. They're keeping her in a drug-induced coma for now to help her heal better. When she wakes up, the first thing she's going to ask for is her son. I have to find him, but I have no idea what to do, other than go to the police."

"That's exactly what you *should* do. It's been, what, around eighteen hours since the kid went missing? That's an eternity in cases like this. When will you be able to get out of here?"

She made a face. "Tomorrow."

Aaron didn't recall making a conscious decision; the words came out of his mouth all on their own. "I'll take care of getting the police started today."

It was a no-brainer, really, on more than one level. There was the personal man-woman level that would have had him licking her boots if she'd asked. On the cop level, there was a scary similarity to the case he was currently working on, which involved children stolen from their families and sold into slavery, mostly overseas.

How convenient was it that he'd come here seeking information about that child-stealing creep Charlie Howard and run into a woman whose child was missing?

Aaron didn't believe in coincidence, not when it came to chasing after bad guys. Even if the missing child in this case had nothing to do with Charlie, there was a reason why he'd been brought to this room, to this woman. At some point that reason would become clear. Meanwhile, he wanted to help find the boy. He could get the investigation started today.

"Can you? Really? Oh, thank you, Aaron."

The way her smile lit her eyes made him want to lap her up, one long stroke of his tongue at a time.

"LaShonda," Hailey continued, "will be so grateful."

Aaron wanted to ask if *she* would be grateful, too, but he swallowed the words. It was definitely too soon to make an ass of himself. Especially when she was holding something back.

"What aren't you telling me?" he asked her.

Her brow wrinkled. "What do you mean?"

"I mean," he said in his lead-'em-where-you-want-'em-to-go voice, "the man took the boy away, and then she was in the hospital having her face put back together. Why did she only assume the man came back?"

"Why?"

"Yes, why?" he asked.

She made a low growling sound somewhere deep in her throat. "Why? Why…because…because she… When she came to for a few minutes in the hospital, the last thing she remembered, she was uninjured and the man was taking Keenan away. She had no memory of getting the crap beaten out of her, yet when rescue workers found her, she had two broken arms, a broken leg, and Lord knows how many head injuries. We hope when they bring her out of the coma that she'll be able to describe what the man looked like, because he seems like a logical suspect, don't you think?"

Aaron nodded and mulled over everything Hailey had told him. On the surface, it sounded credible. Why, then, did he still feel as if she were leaving something out? Something important.

Chapter 2

The next morning, Hailey woke with a groan. She heard a deep, loud groan inside her head, along with a soft *day-yum*.

Oh, hell. "LaShonda." Hailey blinked her eyes open. "You're still here."

Where else you think I'd be, girlfriend?

Hailey stared grimly at the woman in the next bed. LaShonda's lips did *not* move when she spoke. "Back in your own body. Would that be too much to ask?"

You think I like being stuck inside a white girl? Not on your life, sister. But I'm here, so you're all I've got to help me find Keenan. You still gonna help me?

"I talked to Aaron about it yesterday, didn't I?"

Ah yes, Aaron. He looked like a keeper to me, LaShonda said. *You think he'll really help you?*

"Us. I think he'll help *us*. But either way, when I leave here today, I'm going straight to the police to report Keenan being kidnapped."

LaShonda gasped. *I've tried not to think that word, but he was, wasn't he? Kidnapped.*

"If that man took him like you said he did, then yeah, I'd say *kidnapped* is the word," Hailey said. "We need to figure out how to get you back into your body."

Good luck with that. You think I haven't been trying all night? It seems like the harder I try to move, the more frozen in place I become.

Hailey would have asked a dozen questions, made a hundred suggestions and at least one demand—get out of my head—but just then a cheerful teenager in a candy-striper smock brought in a breakfast tray. Before the girl made it back out the door, a nurse arrived with a sickeningly cheerful "Good morning," singing it out as though it were her own personal morning anthem as she took Hailey's blood pressure, pulse and temperature.

Hailey was relieved to find out that her vital signs were normal. She felt a little stiff and achy—okay, maybe a lot stiff and achy—but otherwise fine. Her mind was certainly clearer than it had been yesterday.

It was nearly noon before things fell together. She was eager to go home, dressed in the borrowed scrubs the nurses provided, and ready for the required wheelchair to carry her to the front door of the hospital. She reached for the phone beside her bed to call for a taxi, but Aaron Trent walked in before she could finish dialing.

She hung up and greeted him.

"What are you doing here again?" she asked, smiling at him, amazed at the way her pulse spiked when he smiled back.

"Thought I'd offer you a ride home."

"You don't have to do that."

"No, but on the drive to your place I can tell you about the file I got them to open for the kid, Keenan."

"Oh, Aaron, thank you." Inside her head, LaShonda practically wept with joy.

The door swung open, and the doctor entered with a large X ray in one hand. He glanced at the wheelchair, then at Hailey. "Oh, no, don't think you get to leave us this soon."

"I thought you said I was fine," Hailey protested.

"I said you *seem* fine, but there was a shadow on that last head X ray we took this morning, so we need to get a new shot to make sure."

"A shadow?" Hailey's mouth turned to cotton. "On my X ray?"

"Yes, ma'am."

She realized with a frown that he had yet to look her in the eye. She could have blood gushing from her head and he wouldn't have noticed. "Doctor?"

"Mmm?" he replied, still distracted.

Hailey glanced at Aaron, who was also frowning at the doctor.

"Humph," he said. "If I didn't know any better, I'd swear that we double-exposed your film—which,

now that we're digital, just doesn't happen—or you
had a friend in there with you."

Jeeze Louise, Hailey thought. Had some out-of-
body form of LaShonda shown up in the X ray?

"LaShonda Joy," Hailey chided the unconscious
woman in the next bed, "have you been playing
around in my X rays?"

The doctor, who looked as if he might have started
shaving sometime during the past six months,
laughed. "I guess it did sound a little crazy. Come on,
Ms. Cameron, let's get a new picture of your head.

The orderly turned Hailey's wheelchair toward
the door and pushed her forward.

Hailey looked back at Aaron. "Do you have time
to wait? I'd really like to talk to you."

"I'm in no hurry," he said. "I'll wait here while
you get your picture taken. Smile and say *lightning*."

While Hailey got her follow-up head X ray, she
tried to think of a legitimate reason to send Aaron on
his way and call for a cab to take her home.

So why was she searching for an excuse to turn
down his offer of a ride home, when she wanted very
much to accept it? Since she had asked him to wait
for her, to help her find Keenan.

She wanted to tell herself that she had only asked
because she needed his help. But she knew better.
Above and beyond that perfectly legitimate reason,
she just flat-out wanted to spend time with him.
Wanted it so badly that it tugged hard and deep inside
her, taking her by surprise with its strength.

Must be a leftover side effect of the lightning, she

thought. That bolt of electricity had left her off balance. That was her story, and she was sticking to it.

The new X rays—they took two, just in case— came out clear, so Hailey and Aaron were soon on their way. Halfway to her apartment Hailey thought to ask, "How do you know where I live?"

"Hey, I'm a detective, remember?"

"Oh. Yeah."

LaShonda laughed inside Hailey's head. *He's gotcha there, white girl.*

"Shut up," Hailey muttered.

"Pardon?" Aaron asked with a frown.

"Sorry. I was talking to myself."

"You seem to do that a lot."

"I do?"

"You remind me of my grandmother."

Feigning outrage, Hailey slapped him on the shoulder with the paperwork the hospital had given her when she checked out. "Are you saying I look like—" She realized that she hadn't looked in a mirror since she'd left her house the day before to go jogging. Considering that she felt as if she'd been run over by a semi, she probably looked as if she had been, too. "Never mind."

Aaron chuckled. "I didn't mean you look like my grandmother, I meant you act like her. She talks to herself, too. At least, that's what it looks like, but she swears she's talking to ghosts, that she can see them, hear them."

Hailey glanced at him from the corner of her eye. "Ghosts?"

"The dearly departed. Earthbound spirits. Whatever you want to call dead people who hang around instead of going off to their great reward or whatever."

"And you let her walk around on her own? When did she have her breakdown?" Hailey was nearer and nearer her own breakdown by the minute.

Aaron laughed. "Wait 'til you meet her. She's sharp as a tack and saner than most people you'll ever know."

Block by block, they drew closer to Hailey's apartment. When they arrived, he parked on the street in front of her building. The 1840s redbrick structure was split into eight apartments, four upstairs, four down. Fortunately the plumbing and electricity were much newer than the building itself.

"Nice place," Aaron told her.

"I like it. The owners live downstairs, so they spend the time and money to keep things in good condition, especially on the outside, but they're pretty good with indoor repairs, too." Listen to me, rattling on like an idiot, she thought. Maybe I really am losing it. "Thanks for the ride home."

"You're welcome."

Hailey placed her hand on the door handle and looked over at him. LaShonda had been right—he looked like a keeper, with his dark brown hair and eyes, that sharp jawline, those taut cheekbones. Not to mention lips that looked designed for kissing.

She swallowed and looked away. "I'd invite you up for a drink or a snack, but truth be told, I'm still pretty much out of it."

"Of course you are," he said.

"Tell your grandmother hello for me," she added.

"I'll be glad to. But it's my grand*father*," he said, as he exited the car, "who used to say that a gentleman always walks a lady to her door."

Hailey got out and stood on the sidewalk while he walked around the car to join her. "He did?" she asked.

"He did. Always," he said. "Every time. No excuses."

Hailey bit back a smile. "Am I to assume that you learned this lesson?"

"Since we're halfway to your door, that would probably be a safe assumption."

It had been a long time since a man had walked Hailey to her door. A long time since she had allowed one to. A long time since the possibility had even arisen. The series of losers she'd dated during the past couple of years had all but ground her interest in the opposite sex into dust.

But at the moment she didn't feel like saying no to this particular man.

She didn't know whether to be thrilled at the idea or run screaming in the opposite direction.

He walked beside her up the sidewalk and stood back while she unlocked the front door.

She turned to thank him and say goodbye but never got the chance.

"After you," he said. "Which unit is yours?" At her enquiring look he added, "*This* is not your door."

"Two-A." She led the way up the wide staircase to the second floor. With every aching step, she wished she'd taken the elevator. So much for trying to look fit.

At her front corner apartment, she once again unlocked the door and stepped inside, then turned again to thank Aaron but stopped abruptly.

At the hospital, she'd known she probably looked like death warmed over, so she hadn't dared to look in a mirror. The scrubs, for which she was admittedly grateful, were a singularly unflattering shade of baby-puke green.

Her recovery time, she'd told herself, would be that much faster if she didn't see firsthand how washed-out she looked. Ignorance, they said, was bliss.

Until it came back and slapped you in the face, which was what it felt like when she accidently caught a glimpse of her reflection in the wall mirror next to the door. The sight that greeted her stopped her heart, then drew a scream from her throat. That was *not* her face in the mirror.

Well, it *was* her face, but it was also LaShonda Martin's face, like a transparent mask laid over Hailey's own.

Both faces, and both voices, screamed.

Aaron's training and instincts shot into action. He jumped in front of Hailey and placed himself between her and whatever danger had terrified her into screaming. In less than a second he had his gun out and aimed at…the mirror? The wall?

"What the hell's going on?" he demanded. He could see every square inch of the entry from where he stood. There was no one there but Hailey and himself. Two steps gave him a complete view of the kitchen, dinette, and living room to his left. Three steps to his right he found a bathroom, then a bedroom. He finished by checking the closets and under the bed. There was not another soul in the place.

"Hailey?" he asked, his heart still thundering.

"I'm sorry." She pressed a hand to her chest. "I was just surprised."

"By what? You sounded like you'd been surprised by your friendly neighborhood axe murderer."

"Oh, come on." She reached deep inside herself for control. "The way I look right now, I'm surprised you and everyone else haven't screamed on sight of me."

He narrowed his gaze and studied her. He looked at her so long that she found herself shifting beneath his stare.

"Was that the first time you've looked in a mirror?"

"Since I got fried? Yes. I'm a mess."

Aaron holstered his weapon, then propped his fists on his hips. "I don't think so."

"I beg your pardon?"

"No matter how good you're used to looking, the way you look right now isn't near bad enough to make you scream like you've just seen a giant wart on the end of your nose. Besides, I don't see you as being vain enough to care that much about your looks. So I ask again, what on earth scared you half to death?"

Hailey took a slow, deep breath.

LaShonda snickered. *Yeah, and don't think I'm not insulted that you'd take one look at me and scream.*

"Shut up," Hailey muttered.

Aaron threw both hands in the air. "Fine. I'll be back in an hour—"

"No," she told him. "I'm sorry. I wasn't talking to you."

"You weren't telling me to shut up?"

"No. As for the screaming, the fact is, I *am* that vain."

"If you weren't telling me to shut up, who were you talking to?"

To a woman who's in a coma back in the hospital, she answered silently. Like he would believe that. *She* didn't believe it, and it was happening to her.

Tell him, LaShonda dared her. *Tell him the truth and see what he's made of. Go on, I dare you.*

"I was talking to this stupid voice I keep hearing in my head," Hailey said.

"Yeah? That's the second time you've told that little voice, the one only you can hear, to shut up since we left the hospital."

"That's because that little voice in my head talks too much."

Hey, white girl, I resent that.

"At the risk of sounding like a broken record," Hailey muttered, "shut up."

"There you go again," Aaron said.

"I'm going to take a shower."

"I'll be back in about an hour to take you to the police station."

"Fine. I assume that's to find a missing child and not to have me arrested for talking to myself."

"I don't think that's against the law."

Before he could blink, Aaron found himself outside her closed door. He tried to recall if he'd ever been put out of a woman's home so gently yet firmly, but, no, he decided this was a first for him. Hailey Cameron was a first for him.

Not the voices she heard. Women who heard voices of people who weren't there were nothing new to him. But a woman who had him volunteering to haul her around town without even hinting she might enjoy the ride, a woman who didn't seem to care one way or the other if she ever saw him again, and still he volunteered? Very definitely something new.

Chapter 3

"We have an errand to run before we go to the police station," Hailey told him when he returned to pick her up and they were back in his car, pulling away from the curb.

"We do?" Aaron asked.

"Yes. We need to go by LaShonda's apartment and find a picture of Keenan for the cops."

Aaron scowled at her.

"What's wrong?" she asked.

"Nothing." He huffed out a breath of disgust. "I should have thought of that myself."

Most of the tornado damage at the two-story Willow Crossing apartment complex—where La-Shonda and one hundred and twenty-seven of her nearest neighbors resided—was confined, structurally speaking, to the upper floor.

Streets in the neighborhood were still blocked off due to downed trees, limbs and other debris. Aaron had to park three blocks away, and then they were forced to walk, giving them a chance to admire the lovely blue tarps and sheet after sheet of plywood covering gaping holes in roofs up and down the street.

With LaShonda giving directions inside Hailey's head, the party of three—two?—proceeded to LaShonda's building, halfway along the front side of the complex, facing the communal courtyard.

The courtyard boasted a small patch of thick grass, a couple of picnic tables and a swimming pool that had surely once been pristine but now was littered with mud, leaves, patio furniture, trash—you name it.

Inside the apartment, the bedroom windows provided a scenic view of the parking lot, currently littered with piles of debris from the storm. Random furniture, crushed and overturned cars, broken trees and limbs of all sizes. What trees were left had had the bark stripped off by the tornado. The parking lot looked like a war zone.

The apartment itself was pretty much a disaster, with half the roof gone, followed by wind and rain damage, and the occasional tree limb or two that had blown in. The hole in the roof was covered with a bright blue tarp to keep out whatever it could until real repairs could be made.

Inside the apartment, so many small things had oddly remained in place: a ceramic set of red-breasted bluebirds on the sill over the sink; a shelf of books and children's CDs on the far wall.

Oh, God, LaShonda wailed in Hailey's head.

Hailey wanted to wail with her, but she swallowed her words of sorrow and sympathy. She couldn't explain herself to Aaron, and the words wouldn't help get things done.

"Okay." Hailey rubbed her hands together. "If I were a picture of Keenan…"

LaShonda sniffed. *You'd be in that photo album next to the CDs. Please, God, let it have survived.* Her tear-filled whisper echoed through Hailey's brain.

Hailey reached for the photo album and found it in perfect condition. Thumbing through the book, she found dozens of pictures of Keenan and La Shonda, and other family members and friends.

"They've got quite a family going here," Hailey said to Aaron.

"Can't be as big as mine," he told her. "What about you? Big family?"

She shook her head. "Just me." She sounded so pitiful, even to her own ears, that she forced herself to focus on the album. Most of the photos it held were of Keenan. "What an adorable kid."

"He's a winner, all right," Aaron said.

They thumbed through the album until they found a recent five-by-seven they thought would be a good one for the cops and the media, including the Internet, to use.

"We'll make copies," Aaron muttered, glancing around the room. "Does your friend have insurance to take care of this mess?"

Startled, Hailey held her breath. "Insurance? LaShonda? I..."

Yes! LaShonda cried. *Oh, thank God. I hadn't thought of that.*

"Yes," Hailey said. "Yes, she has insurance. As soon as I'm finished at the police station, I'll get in touch with the insurance company and see what they can do to help."

The voice in Hailey's head, the sniffing and soft crying, stopped. Her mind and LaShonda were quiet.

"I hope Ms. Martin knows what a good friend you are."

"It's not that big a deal," Hailey protested.

Ms. Martin's learnin' fast, LaShonda said. *You're the best, white girl.*

For one irrevocable moment, Hailey forgot to watch her words around Aaron and spoke directly to LaShonda. "Just out of curiosity, since you feel free to call me White Girl all the time, I'm guessing you won't mind if I call you Black Girl?"

All sound seemed to be sucked out of the room. For a long moment, not even their breathing broke the silence.

Finally Aaron spoke. "This time you have to tell me what's going on."

Thinking of trying to play dumb one more time, Hailey opened her mouth to deny knowing what he was talking about.

He beat her to the punch. "And don't bother telling me you don't know what I'm talking about. Who are you talking to? Trust me, I've heard it all, so you won't surprise me."

"You say that now," Hailey muttered.

What're you going to do? LaShonda asked her.

Hailey shook her head. "Maybe I'll surprise you after all," she told Aaron. "I'm talking to LaShonda Martin."

"The kid's mother?"

"Yes."

"The woman in the other bed in your hospital room?"

"One and the same."

"But she's not dead. Is she?" he asked, his brow furrowed with obvious concern.

"No, she's not dead. She's in a coma."

"She's in a coma," Aaron repeated. "In the hospital."

"That's right," Hailey assured him.

"She's in a coma, in the hospital," Aaron repeated, and started ticking items off on his fingers. "And you're here, several miles away, and you're talking to her. You can hear her, and I can't. Can you see her?"

"It's complicated," Hailey said.

It's a cop-out, LaShonda said. *You're a wimp, white girl.*

"Will you shut up?" Hailey demanded. "I'm telling him, aren't I?"

Aaron rubbed his hands together like a pirate getting ready to count his booty. "Oh, this is going to be good, I can tell."

"You enjoy watching someone have a breakdown right before your eyes?" Hailey said. Her hands were shaking.

"A breakdown?"

"That's what they call it when a person starts hearing voices, isn't it?" she asked.

"Or maybe that's what they call it when you try to change the subject and avoid answering the question."

"I'm not trying to change the subject." Hailey took a deep breath to calm her nerves. "It's just that nothing like this has ever happened to me before. It's a little unsettling."

"Nothing like what? Like hearing voices?"

"Yes. But it's really only one voice." She decided to ignore the moment back in the hospital when she'd known quite clearly that he was thinking about her naked.

"LaShonda Joy Martin."

"That's right. My hospital roomie."

"She's in a coma, but she can talk to you? How does that work?" Aaron asked.

He was way too accepting of the idea of her hearing voices. He should be skeptical, at the least, rather than looking her up and down, making her spine tingle. Why wasn't he laughing at her, or scoffing, or shaking his head and walking away? Just because his grandmother claimed to talk to ghosts? He didn't really believe *her*, did he?

"Talk to me, Hailey. Tell me what's going on."

"It happened at the hospital," she said. Once she started, the words wouldn't stop. She told him all she and LaShonda knew, or guessed, about how the other woman's spirit had ended up inside her head.

"How long have you known each other?"

"Now you're talking like a cop, trying to put

words in my mouth. LaShonda and I have never met. I mean, we never even heard of each other until they hooked me up to that oxygen machine. I inhaled, and there she was, talking from inside my head."

"So she's not a ghost."

"That's right."

"Okay," he said. "Let's get to the police station so you can file a report about the boy."

Keenan. His name is Keenan, LaShonda said.

"LaShonda says his name is Keenan."

"Right. Sorry. We'll stop on the way to the station and make copies of Keenan's photo so we can put the original back."

"That's all you have to say? I tell you I have conversations with a coma patient, and you say we'll stop and make copies?"

"Hmm. You're right." He grabbed her gently by the shoulders and kissed her hard and quick. He gave her a grin. "This is where I'm supposed to ask if you're crazy. Are you having a breakdown? Going schizo on me?"

Hailey sputtered. He'd kissed her, and now he was all but laughing at her. Hailey stiffened her shoulders and turned toward the door. She might not be going schizo, but any moment she was going to start drooling. "Let's get to the police station before I start to drool."

He laughed as he followed her out the door and down the stairs.

They made color copies of Keenan's photo, then drove to the police station. Aaron was treated by everyone there as one of their own.

Hailey didn't know what to think of this man who rolled so easily with whatever punches came his way. Punches such as a complete stranger who talked to herself. He acted as if she was normal, the day was normal, and everything was right with the world.

He led her into a large open room filled with desks and what sounded like two million ringing telephones. They stopped beside a desk near the back corner, and Aaron introduced her to Officer Mike Fontain, who had already started the paperwork for Keenan based on Aaron's input earlier. Now, with Hailey's information, especially Keenan's photo, they could move ahead.

Hailey gave Officer Fontain all the information she had and, with LaShonda's help, answered all his questions. They worked for a time with a sketch artist until they had a vague picture of the suspect. It wasn't much, because LaShonda couldn't remember the man's face.

"All right." Fontain pushed back his chair and stood. "Hope Howard's not in on this. We'll get this photo out, and we'll add it to the Amber Alert right away."

"You've already put out an Amber Alert?" Hailey asked.

"As soon as Aaron came in yesterday afternoon," Fontain told her.

Inside Hailey's head, LaShonda gushed her thanks at the officer and begged Hailey to kiss the man and worship at his feet, if he would only find her baby boy.

Hailey smiled but otherwise ignored her.

Once they were all back in Aaron's car, he offered

to buy lunch. Because she was hungry, Hailey accepted. She told herself it had nothing to do with not being ready to leave his company.

Hailey was usually comfortable being alone. She considered herself an independent woman, more than capable of taking care of herself. Most of the time she preferred her own company to anyone else's. She saw plenty of people at work, and that was enough socializing for her. Especially since she'd caught her boyfriend of two years ago, dear ol' Randy, cheating on her with one of her best friends, dear ol' Donna. Hailey hadn't been the most open or trusting person since then.

Yet today she didn't want to be alone. She found Aaron interesting, wanted to trust him. *Did* trust him.

When would she ever learn?

Maybe it was because she had come close to dying, or realizing how lucky she was compared to LaShonda. Or maybe it was simply the magnetic pull of the man behind the wheel.

"Where were you thinking of eating?" she asked.

"I'm not sure. Let me check something." He placed a call on his cell phone. "Hey, beautiful, what's on the menu today?" He lowered the phone and looked at Hailey. "How's your cholesterol?"

"My cholesterol's normal to low. How's yours?"

"Mine's fine and dandy. You up for the world's greatest pork chops, breaded and fried, with fried okra, mashed potatoes and the equally sinful works?"

"It sounds delicious."

"We're on our way," he said into the phone.

"Two for lunch. I'm not going to be seeing my brothers or sisters, am I? Great. Thanks. Be there in twenty." He disconnected and clipped the phone back to his belt.

"No brothers or sisters? Where are we going?" Hailey asked, her heart speeding at their teasing banter.

"How freaked out are you going to be when I tell you I'm taking you to my grandmother's for lunch?"

Even LaShonda fell silent at that.

Claudia Jean Trent lived in a beautiful old two-story Victorian in the quiet countryside beyond the Baton Rouge city limits. Tall, glossy-green magnolia trees decorated the huge yard, with rows and pools of flowers—reds, yellows, whites, purples—and shrubs ranging from dark to light green in various beds around the house, up and down the front yard, following every curve, every bend, every sidewalk.

There was enough work here, Hailey thought, to keep a full-time gardener busy on the flowers alone. She sincerely hoped Aaron's grandmother had regular help.

Aaron barreled up the circular gravel drive and parked near the front door. By the time he exited the car, rounded the hood and opened the passenger door for her, the cloud of gravel dust raised by the car had wafted away in the warm southern breeze.

He opened the front door without knocking, just stepped inside and took Hailey with him.

Sudden nervousness seized her. He had brought her home to meet his grandmother. What did it mean? This couldn't be the same as a guy taking her home to meet his mother, surely. They hadn't known each other that long, or in that way.

So what *was* this all about?

"Aaron, why are we here?" she asked quietly in the doorway before anyone saw them.

Oh, sister, why do you want to rock that boat? LaShonda cried.

"What do you mean?" Aaron asked. "We're here for lunch."

LaShonda gave out a hoot.

"Come on," Hailey told him. "We could have eaten lunch anywhere, but you bring me to your grandmother's. I figure you must have a reason for bringing me here other than her pork chops."

He placed his hands lightly on her shoulders and looked at her for a long moment. Long enough to make Hailey want to squirm.

"All right," he said. "I wanted you to meet Gran. When you do, I think you'll see why."

"Why don't you just tell me?"

"You know that voice you hear in your head?"

"LaShonda," Hailey said, defiant, daring him to argue that she was making it all up.

"Gran is going to understand what you're experiencing."

As if hearing her cue, Claudia Jean Trent stepped into the entry hall. "There you are, Aaron, dear." She reached out to hug her grandson.

"Gran." He returned the hug.

Hailey smiled and looked on. At a guess, Aaron was around thirty-five, so his grandmother must be about seventy-five. She looked more like sixty, with salt-and-pepper hair, smiling blue eyes and enough wrinkles around her face to give the impression of a life well-lived, filled with her share of both pain and laughter.

"Who have you brought with you, dear?" She turned toward Hailey, and her smile froze in place. "Oh, my heavens. Pardon me for asking, but do you know you're not, uh, not alone?"

"You can see her?" Hailey asked, her heart racing.

You can see me? LaShonda asked at the same moment, with a quiver in her voice.

"I can see both of you, which I'm sure is why my number-three grandson brought you to me, isn't that right, Aaron, dear? Why don't you run off to the kitchen and get us each a tall glass of sweet tea, while this lovely lady—both lovely ladies—come with me to the parlor, so we can get to know each other." She turned and threaded her arm through Hailey's. "I'm just dying to hear how you ended up this way."

Hailey felt as if a whirlwind had swept through the house and rearranged things to suit Mrs. Trent's wishes. Before Hailey could blink or LaShonda could comment, they found themselves in what must have been the parlor in question. The room looked out over the front yard. Drapes, walls and furniture all gleamed in white and gold, with turquoise accents. Definitely a woman's room. A lady's room. Dainty and spotless.

"My goodness, where are my manners? I didn't even give poor Aaron a chance to introduce us. I'm Claudia Jean Trent. You can call me Claudia Jean. And you are?"

"I'm Hailey Cameron."

I'm LaShonda Joy Martin. Can you really see me? Can you hear me, too?

"Yes, I can." Claudia smiled. "How did you end up in there? Are you dead, sweetheart?"

"No," Hailey responded.

No, LaShonda said. *I'm in a coma, at the hospital.*

Hailey smiled. A small sense of relief filled her, the first since realizing she was no longer alone in her own head. "And you can speak for yourself."

How about that? I can.

It took only a few minutes for Hailey and LaShonda to explain their situation to Claudia. Halfway through the telling, Aaron brought in a round of tall glasses of sweet iced tea, and a tray of carrot sticks, stuffed celery, cauliflower and broccoli and joined the women.

"What can they do, Gran?" he asked when the tale was told.

"Seems to me they're doing it already. They've both received medical attention, they've accepted that they are, shall we say, psychically joined. They've got you and the police looking for the child, and you've started securing LaShonda's belongings."

"But we can't seem to separate," Hailey pointed out.

"Ah, yes, there is that," Claudia said. "Why do you think you can't return to your own body, LaShonda?"

Hailey could practically feel LaShonda blushing beneath Claudia's steady gaze.

Well, if I knew that, LaShonda griped, *don't you think I'd do it?*

"Would you?" Claudia asked.

Hailey gnawed on the inside of her jaw to keep from butting in and blaming LaShonda for staying in her body to force her into searching for Keenan. As if Hailey could have turned away from such a plea from a woman who, at present, had no way to help herself.

Of course I would. On the other hand, if I go back to my body and get stuck in the hospital, who's going to remind white girl here to keep looking for my son?

"I see." Claudia took a sip of tea and sat back in her seat. "I can understand that."

"Is she giving you a line about needing to make sure Hailey keeps looking for her kid?" Aaron asked.

A small chuckle of laughter slipped from Hailey's mouth. "I forgot. This time you're the only one in the room who's different. Now everybody can hear La-Shonda except you."

He rolled his eyes. "That's nothing new around here, believe me."

"I beg your pardon?" she asked.

"Ladies," Claudia called. "Come out and meet our guests."

"Wha—" But that was as far as Hailey got before two figures shimmered into view, as if generated by the wave of a moviemaker's magic special effects wand. First a faint outline, then it started to fill in, fading and glowing, fading and glowing, until each figure settled into a steady visual image standing on either side of Claudia's chair.

Suddenly they were no longer glimmering images. As if Scotty had beamed them up, they were women, solid flesh-and-blood bodies. Hailey could see their chests rise and fall beneath their period costumes. One woman wore a soft gingham dress trimmed in white ruffles, while the other dressed in dire black, with her dark hair pulled back sharply from her face into a tight bun at her nape.

"So," Claudia said to Hailey, "you can see them."

Hailey swallowed. "Wh-who?"

I see them, LaShonda stated. *Who are they?*

The woman in black sighed. "More people to talk about us as if we're not here, Claudia? How tedious."

Oh, we see you, all righty, LaShonda shot back, *so you can just wipe that attitude off your face.*

"Hush up," Hailey warned. If she could have, she would have jerked on LaShonda's arm. She had the feeling that Aaron thought his grandmother might be able to help them in some way. She didn't want to make her mad by having LaShonda's mouth running off at her...friends.

The woman in black stiffened, perhaps in offense.

Claudia chuckled. "It's all right, Hailey. I can't recall the last time anyone but me could see or hear Marva or Mrs. Porterman."

"I don't understand," Hailey said, her nerves clacking.

"I imagine it is a tad confusing," Claudia said.

"Ah, Gran, the master of understatement." On their own, Aaron's words might have stung. They were, however, said with a smile and followed by a wink.

None of which did anything to help Hailey understand what was going on.

"You didn't tell her," Claudia said.

He reached over and touched the back of his grandmother's hand. The smile in his eyes softened. "Not everything. It's yours to tell, Gran, not mine."

"Smart boy," Claudia told Aaron. "You bring me this lovely young woman, and she brings me her friend. Both of them can see and hear my friends. You might want to keep this one."

"Gran," Aaron warned, "let's get back to the subject. Both of you can see things other people can't. Hailey's ability started when she was struck by lightning the other day."

"And LaShonda's alive but in a coma," Claudia said thoughtfully. "That's a new one on me. Maybe it's because of the drugs they're using to keep you unconscious?"

If I'm new to you, LaShonda said, *that means they're...dead?*

"Yes," Claudia said.

"But...how can that be?" Hailey asked.

I'd say, when you're dead, you're gone, LaShonda said. *But then, here I am, hanging out inside a white girl, so what do I know?*

"Sometimes," Claudia said, "the spirit of a dead person simply isn't ready, or willing, to leave, to go...wherever it's supposed go. Sometimes it needs help, or needs to offer help. That's what people like you and I are for," she said to Hailey.

"To help them?" Hailey asked, not sure she was ready or willing to accept such a responsibility.

Like, to help me find my Keenan, LaShonda said.

"That's right," Claudia agreed.

"While we're doing that," Aaron said, "maybe one of your ghosts will help me find Charlie Howard."

"Who is he?" Hailey asked.

"He's that guy I told you I'm looking for. His aunt is the woman you jog past every day. The one we talked about."

From there the conversation traveled from the fancy parlor to the comfortable eat-in kitchen, where Claudia served the salad. While they ate, she checked the pork chops in the oven and the vegetables on the stove.

She agreed with Hailey that LaShonda needed to return to her own body. Marva and Mrs. Porterman recalled the days shortly after their own passings the only things they could compare to her coma. They remembered how weak they had been, how disoriented. It had been weeks, months, before they'd felt in control of themselves and learned how to navigate through the new dimension in which they found themselves. How to live with the frustration of not being seen or heard by anyone but Claudia Jean and an old hound that lived in the barn.

"LaShonda doesn't have weeks or months," Hailey said. "In a day or two they're going to pull her out of her coma and someone needs to be in there." She tapped a finger to the side of her head.

"From what Marva and Mrs. Porterman went through," Claudia Jean said, "the best thing to me would be relaxing. Both of you. That might help LaShonda ease back into her own body."

The two ghosts agreed.

Relaxing sounded easier said than done, when so

much counted on it, but Hailey and LaShonda agreed to give it their best that afternoon.

After the meal, everyone helped clean up, then Hailey, LaShonda and Aaron headed back to town.

"What do you think?" They were a mile from his grandmother's house before Aaron spoke.

"I think your Gran truly loves you, to allow you to show up with our kind of trouble," Hailey said.

"But did it help?" He couldn't believe how much her answer mattered. How much he wanted to be able to help her. "Can you use anything she and her pals had to say?"

Hailey chuckled. "Her pals? Oh, God, they would love that."

"You're not angry with me for butting in on your and LaShonda's problem?"

"Never." She reached out and covered the back of his hand with hers, where he gripped the gearshift. "I'm grateful," she said, giving his hand a slight squeeze. "I know what to do now. And I know I'm not losing my mind. That I'm not the only person who hears voices. That LaShonda's not the only invisible person floating around."

Without thinking, Aaron turned his hand and threaded his fingers through hers. "You're not losing your mind, and you're not going through this alone."

"I'm not?"

"You're not."

"Thank you." She squeezed his hand again. "When you drop me off at my car, I'm going straight to the hospital and give LaShonda a chance to relax."

Chapter 4

Except for the hum and beep of life-affirming machines, dusk was quiet in LaShonda's hospital room.

In the morning the doctor was going to bring LaShonda slowly out of her coma.

Hailey could feel LaShonda's spirit relaxing. The visit to Aaron's grandmother had given the other woman the confidence she needed to let go of Hailey and return to her own body. Thank God for that, Hailey thought. Thank God for Aaron and his family.

Somehow, throughout lunch, Hailey had managed to learn more than a little about the Trent family. First, it was large. She wasn't even certain how many brothers and sisters Aaron had, but there were several. Then came the aunts and uncles and cousins, at least half of whom had children of their own.

Hailey had been an only child of older parents, each one also an only child. They'd died before she reached her teens. Foster care had bounced her around until she had aged out of the system.

She'd never had a roommate—except at a foster home.

She'd never had a best friend.

She'd never had a brother or sister, never gotten close enough to any of her foster siblings to think of them that way.

She once developed a crush on one of her older so-called foster brothers and learned quickly enough not to trust boys.

She had learned that she was her own best friend, and she liked it that way.

Maybe those things helped explain why she had taken to LaShonda as well as she had. They'd been together less than two days, but it felt much more permanent to Hailey than anything she'd known as a child. Yes, she looked forward to recovering her privacy, but having someone to talk to whenever she wanted was a heady thing. Sort of like a best friend and sister rolled into one.

Maybe she had been lonely after all.

Not that she thought LaShonda necessarily returned the sentiment. The woman had her own family and, undoubtedly, friends. In fact, tomorrow should see the arrival of an aunt from New Orleans, who would look after LaShonda while she mended and help her get her home and life back together as the police searched for Keenan.

Thoughts of Keenan brought thoughts of Aaron.

To Hailey's shame, Aaron quickly crowded the young boy from her mind. Tomorrow she would start seeing what she could do to help search for Keenan, but she had to go back to work at the restaurant tomorrow evening.

For now, she would let herself think of large, loving families who produced intriguing men such as Aaron Trent. If she let herself, she could still feel the taut skin across the back of his hand where it rested on the gearshift knob. His warmth had surprised her. She'd been even more surprised when he had turned his hand and threaded his fingers through hers. The mere memory weakened her joints.

You're thinking of him, aren't you?

Hailey gave a start. "LaShonda? You sound different. Are you all right?"

Good way to change the subject, girlfriend, but I'm back where I belong, if that's what you mean.

It took a moment for Hailey to realize what LaShonda meant, and then…

Hailey had expected that once she had her body back to herself once more, that feeling of loneliness she never let herself acknowledge would seep back in again. If she were honest, she had to admit it was one reason why she stood at the entrance to a popular restaurant and greeted the diners every evening. Faux family.

Looking at things now, she could see that it was the reason she jogged three miles every other day— to outrun the emptiness.

That it was the reason she stopped and visited with an elderly lady over a glass of lemonade mid-run—to relieve someone else's loneliness as well as her own.

But for the past couple of days she had felt the need for neither the diners nor the jogging. She'd had Aaron to share herself with. And she'd had LaShonda. Temporary, both of them, to be sure, but she'd had them. It was surprising how good that felt.

Not so surprising was the burning in her eyes and the closing of her throat when relief for LaShonda swamped her. The fear had been larger than Hailey had realized that LaShonda would not be able to return to her own body. Ever.

Fear of losing Aaron still weighed like a ball of ice in her gut, but the fear of sharing her mind with LaShonda forever was gone. In the odd mixture of remaining fear and sheer relief, Hailey's composure crumbled.

It was late when Aaron finally made it to the hospital to check on Hailey. He hadn't meant—hadn't wanted—to leave her there alone with LaShonda so long, but he'd wasted two hours trying to connect with a particular informant who might have a line on Charlie. He'd also tried again to reach the elderly lady Hailey jogged past every day. No luck there, either.

The air-conditioned interior of the hospital revived him from the heat of the day. He pushed open the door to LaShonda's room and nearly fell to his knees.

The light was low, and all he heard over the quiet beeping and whooshing of the machines that carried LaShonda through her coma was the soft weeping of a woman.

Without question, he knew it was Hailey.

When his eyes adjusted to the dim light, he saw her, slumped in her chair, shoulders shaking, face and fists buried in the bedding at LaShonda's hip.

Thinking the worst had happened, his heart filled with dread.

"Hailey!" He rushed to her side and slipped his arms around her. "Hailey, honey, what's wrong? Did we lose her? Talk to me. Is she gone?"

"Gone? No, no. She's good. She's fine. She's back."

He was too busy nuzzling his nose into the warmth of her neck to realize what she was saying at first, and then it hit him.

"What?"

"She's back."

"You mean…back? As in, back in her own body?"

"Ye-yes."

Aaron's heart rate settled slightly at the news. Still, her tears touched something inside him that he'd thought never to feel. He hadn't known he even had that soft spot deep inside. "Then why are you crying?"

"Relief. I was afraid she wouldn't be able to get back to herself in time."

"In time?"

"The doctor's coming in the morning to start pulling her out of the coma."

"Doesn't sound like fun. Are you going to be here for that?" he asked.

She started to pull away and sit up, but he tucked her head into the crook of his neck and held her closer, as if they sat this way every day.

She shifted around, then finally settled. "Yes.

Seven a.m. Shirley, her aunt, is coming up from New Orleans to be here for her."

"You sound exhausted," he said. She felt more frail than he'd realized, too.

"I wasn't tired until LaShonda said she'd made it back. Then I just…went limp, I guess."

"No wonder," he told her. "With the way you've been going these past couple of days. Why don't I take you home so you can get some rest?"

"I haven't done anything but sit around," she protested.

"Yeah, with another person hanging out in your head. That, plus getting struck by lightning, plus spending the night in a strange place, where nurses wake you up at regular intervals to make sure you're asleep. Then you go through a tornado-damaged building. Then you have lunch with ghosts. And that was only half your day."

"Okay." She laughed. "I think I'm too tired to argue."

"There. You admitted it," he said. "You're tired. LaShonda, I'm taking her out of here for a while. We'll be back in the morning, when they turn off your juice and bring you out of hiding. I've never had injuries as severe as yours, but I've had my share, so trust me, you're going to want to ask for more drugs. Lots of drugs."

Against his shoulder, Hailey shuddered. "You never said why you're not a cop anymore. Did you end up with a drug habit from your hospital stay?"

He pulled her to her feet and walked her toward the door. "No, no drug habit, from the hospital or elsewhere. I took one to the shoulder. Tore up my rotator cuff and cost me too much range of motion to pass the annual physical."

"Took one? You mean…you were shot?"

"Yeah. It happens now and then in my line of work."

"I'm sorry. It must have been hard to accept the loss of your job."

"Yeah, it's been hard. But it might not be permanent," he said. "If I can find the right therapy to get my range of motion back, I might be able to pass the physical again."

"Really?" She raised her head from his shoulder and looked up at him.

Aaron met her gaze with wonder. Her eyes glowed like a small child's at Christmas, having been told that Santa was on the roof.

"Why do you care so much?" he asked.

She ducked her head and looked away. "It's in your eyes, how much you think of yourself as a cop."

With one finger to her chin, Aaron turned her head and peered down into her bright blue eyes. "You're pretty observant."

"It's what I do, observe people."

"You do? Why is it that the only thing I seem to know about you is that you work at Chez Gigi?"

"You know that much? I don't know why you don't know more. We've been best friends for, what, less than thirty-six hours?"

Outside, the parking lot was well lit. He walked her to the passenger door of his car and opened it with a flourish that would have been grand if he'd worn a cape. "Your chariot awaits. Hop in and I'll take you home."

"My car's over there." She nodded toward her small car, parked another ten yards away.

"I'll take you home and bring you back in the morning," he offered.

"Thank you, but that's too much trouble for you, plus it leaves me stranded at home if I decide I want to go out tonight."

He leaned one arm on the open door of his car. "If you're too tired to drive…"

"I'm fine, really," she offered.

"If you say so," he said as he walked her to her car. "I'll just follow you home to make sure."

"I wonder what that says about you, that you would go to the trouble," she said. "I wonder what it says about me, that I don't seem to mind. If anybody but you said they were going to follow me home, I'd accuse them of stalking."

"It says that you have excellent sense."

Hailey chuckled. "Says you."

Aaron's cell phone rang. He pulled it from the case on his belt loop and read the text message on the screen. "I guess my stalking days are over, at least for now," he told Hailey.

She reached for him. He stepped into her embrace and hugged her.

"You have to work?" she asked.

"An informant has some information on Charlie Howard."

"Your bail-jumping child stealer?"

"That's the one. You'll be here in the morning

for LaShonda?" he asked. He ran his hand up and down her arm.

"At seven, yes. You?" She wanted to curl up against him and let whatever happened happen.

"I'll be here," he said. "I won't be able to stay long, but I'll be here in case she wakes up with perfect memory of the man who took Keenan."

"I won't be able to stay long, either," she admitted. "I have to go back to work tomorrow at four. Before that, I want to see if there's anything I can do to help look for Keenan. And I'm going to start jogging again."

"Do yourself a favor and check the weather first, please."

"Don't remind me. I'm trying not to think about lightning, or I might be too scared to run."

"Think about this instead." He turned her in his arms until they were aligned chest to chest. Their mouths met, tasted, toyed with each other. Then they parted and said good-night.

The first thing Hailey did when she made it home was sleep. She dreamed of kissing Aaron. When she woke it was the middle of the night, and she felt slightly disoriented. She had her life back. She knew she had to go to work that evening, even looked forward to it. But for now, she was alone with her thoughts.

Her thoughts turned to LaShonda. She was looking forward to being there for the next step in LaShonda's recovery.

She wondered what it said about her that she was looking forward even more to seeing Aaron again.

* * *

7:00 a.m. came at its usual time, and Hailey was at the hospital a few minutes early. She turned the last corner before LaShonda's room, and there stood Aaron. At the sight of him, her heart jolted.

"Hey," she said in greeting. It was so good to see him.

"Morning." He stood back and allowed her to enter the room before him.

She paused in the doorway, her shoulder brushing his chest. She could feel his gaze on her and couldn't help but look up at him. When their gazes met, she felt the remnants of lightning dancing down her spine.

A sound from near LaShonda's bed drew their attention. They tore their gazes apart and stepped through the doorway.

The room was already so crowded, Hailey was afraid someone would throw them out. She saw one doctor, three nurses and a woman who had to be LaShonda's Aunt Shirley, whom Hailey had met by phone the day before. Add Hailey and Aaron, and LaShonda herself, and the head count peaked at eight. That was a lot for such a small room. Thankfully the second bed was still empty.

Hailey probably should have hugged the wall to keep from getting in anyone's way, but she needed to let LaShonda know she was there. So she made a place for herself at the bedside opposite the doctor and touched LaShonda's free hand.

"I'm here, girlfriend, just like I promised. Aaron's with me, and Aunt Shirley's here to take care of you.

Now it's your turn to do your thing and wake up when the doctor says, okay?"

She squeezed LaShonda's hand again, then stepped back toward the wall. Instead of a cool, solid wall at her back, she felt a warm, sculpted chest. Two strong arms wrapped around her and pulled her close. Her heart stumbled.

For fear Aaron would let go of her if she so much as breathed, she stood still and stared as the doctor fiddled with the IV in LaShonda's arm.

In a short time, LaShonda groaned. Her eyes blinked open. They were the color of dark coffee, and filled with pain and tears. Her lips, nostrils, eyes and ears were swollen and the only things not covered by white bandages. She looked straight at Hailey, and her eyes slowly blinked again. Her lips moved.

Hailey leaned forward and touched LaShonda's hand again. Aaron moved, too, staying pressed against Hailey's back.

"LaShonda, it's me, Hailey."

"White girl," Hailey managed to say through cracked lips.

Relief flooded Hailey. LaShonda remembered the time she'd spent out of her body. How miraculous, Hailey thought.

She repeated to LaShonda what she'd said mere moments ago, letting her know specifically that Aunt Shirley was there for her. "You made it, girlfriend."

"Day-yum."

Hailey laughed. "That's right. Day-yum."

And then LaShonda closed her eyes and fell sound asleep.

* * *

As they left the hospital room together sometime later, Hailey wanted badly to think of a reason not to part company with Aaron, but she couldn't think of one. The independent woman in her insisted she was glad they weren't going to be together for the rest of the day. She didn't need a man in her life. She was more than capable of taking care of herself. She earned enough at her job to support herself in a comfortable style. She was more than content with her own company. She even liked to travel alone.

Her happiness did not depend on anyone other than herself.

A man was handy now and then for sex and for moving heavy furniture.

If only she could believe herself.

Chapter 5

Hailey and Aaron parted company in the hospital parking lot. He had to check in with the district attorney's office. Hailey had to do…something.

Jog. She wanted to jog. She felt the need to stretch her muscles and exercise her lungs. To run away from these conflicting feelings of needing to stand on her own and wanting to lean on—and lap up—Aaron Trent.

She threw on a pair of running shorts and shoes, and an oversize New Orleans Saints T-shirt. She clipped a bottle of water and her cell phone and keys onto her belt loops, and trotted out the door.

Outside, the morning sun burned the bare skin of her forearms. She made a U-turn and slathered on plenty of sunscreen, then hit the sidewalk again.

The sky was a clear summer blue. Not a bolt of lightning in sight.

She stretched out her legs and hit her stride in less than a block. She started out on her usual route, with plans to cut it in half and jog only one and a half miles this first time out after a couple of days off.

A few blocks later she neared Mrs. Shelton's house, hoping the woman was home and offering her usual lemonade.

She was one house away when she was hit by disappointment at finding the front porch empty. No sweet gray-haired lady, no sweaty pitcher of lemonade beside two gleaming glasses. Not plastic cups, but crystal glasses. Mrs. Shelton's motto was Only the Best.

Hailey forced herself to maintain her pace as she jogged past the house.

A loud crash from inside stopped her cold. Two voices, a man's and a woman's, rose in anger. Another crash.

Hailey started up the sidewalk. At the front door, she rang the bell and pounded on the door.

"Mrs. Shelton? It's Hailey, Mrs. Shelton. Are you all right?"

No answer.

"If I don't get an answer, Mrs. Shelton, I'm calling 911."

The response was barely audible. "I'm fine."

Hailey called 911 anyway and explained the situation, adding that Aaron Trent with the district attorney's office was looking for the woman who lived there. Then she pounded on the door again and tried the doorknob, which turned beneath her hand, so she let herself in.

The door slammed back at her, and hit her hard in the head and shoulder. Hailey stumbled and cried out.

"Interfering bitch," a man snarled.

Hailey put to use all the various self-defense classes she'd taken over the years, kicking out sideways and taking him hard in the thigh.

Damn. A few inches short of her mark.

Across the room, Mrs. Shelton struggled to get to her feet. A trickle of blood streamed down one temple.

Outraged on behalf of the woman, Hailey whirled on the assailant. "You bastard." This time she aimed her fists at his head. "Who do you think you are?" She hit him again with a jab to his shoulder.

He hit back with a punch to her face that knocked her into the end table beside the sofa. When she straightened, he was swinging at Mrs. Shelton with a knife.

The older woman screamed, "Charlie, no!"

"Shut up, Auntie, and gimme my damn key." He lunged and sliced her arm open from shoulder to elbow.

Oh, God, Hailey thought. This was the nephew Aaron was after. The bail jumper. The child stealer.

She threw herself at his back and pulled with all her strength to get him away from his aunt. She managed to knock the knife from his hand. He dove for it, but she held on to him, making him fall short of his goal by bare inches.

They rolled across the floor, trading punches, crashing into furniture. Sheer terror kept Hailey from giving in to the pain of his blows.

Charlie got his hands on his knife again and lunged toward his aunt, with Hailey wrapped around his legs.

"No!" Hailey cried. She managed to pull him back just barely enough to keep him from stabbing his aunt.

He kicked out with one boot and caught her in the chest, knocking the breath out of her.

There was a loud crash and a scramble of voices. Hailey knew she was losing it, because one of the voices sounded like Aaron. She gasped harder to bring air into her tortured lungs. Please, God, just... one...breath.

"Easy, baby."

A familiar hand reached for her arm.

"Just breathe. In and out, real slow. Don't panic. Just breathe. It'll happen, baby, don't be afraid."

If strength of will could make a difference, she would breathe again. She would do whatever it took to keep feeling that hand on her arm. Her gasping breath wheezed in and out of her throat so loudly that she could barely hear him, but Aaron's voice soothed her enough to allow her airways to relax in small stages. They had to relax, because if she couldn't breathe again, she would die. And if she died, she would never feel Aaron's touch or hear his voice again.

"That's it, baby," he told her. "Stay with me and just breathe. That's it."

Finally, slowly, Hailey managed to drag enough air into her lungs to make her think she perhaps wasn't going to die after all.

When Aaron realized she was breathing, he

lowered his forehead to her shoulder and started shaking. Damn, he'd nearly lost her. He barely knew her, but he knew enough about her to want to know more. Time and time again she put herself out for the sake of others. LaShonda, Keenan, Mrs. Shelton.

When was the last time someone put her first? When was the last time she allowed such a thing? He wanted, he realized as her breathing settled to normal, to be the person she let get close to her.

"Aaron."

"Thank God," he said fiercely.

"You came." She struggled to sit up.

He shifted her until she sat and leaned against him, then held on as tightly as he could without hurting her. Around them, the room was in chaos, with police and EMTs everywhere. Charlie Howard, being handcuffed and dragged out the door, was cussing a blue streak. His aunt, Wynona Shelton, five feet from where Hailey and Aaron sat, moaned quietly while the EMTs stanched the bleeding from the long cut on her arm, and the several cuts on her hands and face.

Hailey looked worried. "Is she going to be all right?"

"Looks like it," Aaron said. "I'll check when they've had a few more minutes with her."

"Hailey?" the older woman called weakly.

"Mrs. Shelton? I'm over here. Are you all right?"

"Am I all right, young man?" she asked the EMT.

"You're going to be right as rain, ma'am. Just a few cuts that will probably pain you some for a bit. And we need to take you in for some X rays and to check for any internal injuries, or maybe a mild concussion."

"My. Did you hear all of that, Hailey?" Mrs. Shelton asked faintly.

"I did. I'll come by the hospital and check on you, so you do what they tell you, all right?"

"Yes, dear."

After a few minutes the EMTs lifted Mrs. Shelton onto a gurney and wheeled her out of the house.

"Oh, thank God." Hailey went limp in Aaron's arms as she watched Mrs. Shelton being carried away and let relief wash through her veins. The steely warmth of Aaron's arms around her gave her the security she needed—security she hadn't realized she lacked or longed for—to release the tight rein she usually held on her emotions and let her tears free.

"I hardly ever cry," she managed to say between sobs.

"You go ahead and cry all you want," he told her, rubbing his hand up and down her back. "Just keep breathing."

"It's like all I ever do is cry around you."

Aaron held her close and let her cry. Her tears opened a yawning hole deep inside and pulled him in.

Dear God, he'd almost lost her before he'd even realized how important she was to him.

"Not true, not true. You're no crybaby. Today you were Wonder Woman."

The next few hours went by in a fog for Hailey. EMTs poked and prodded her. Aaron encouraged them, over her objections, to take her to the hospital.

She lost that argument. She barely even remembered it a few minutes later.

Sometime after that, there were nurses, a doctor, and more poking and prodding. A bandage here and there. A prescription for painkillers. Swallow this antibiotic. A call to her boss to say she wouldn't be in that night.

She remembered spending an eternity in the waiting area for word on Mrs. Shelton, with occasional forays to see LaShonda, who was still sleeping, this time thanks to painkillers and plain old exhaustion. Aaron was with Hailey every step of the way.

"Why don't I take you home?" he offered when they came back from LaShonda's room. "You're exhausted. Let me drive you home." He looked at her quizzically. "Why are you smiling?"

"I don't get babied often," she said. "It's kind of fun."

He brushed a finger across her cheek and smiled. "I'm glad to be of service."

"Why don't you be of further service and find out how much longer it'll be before we can see Mrs. Shelton?"

"Now you're taking advantage of my willingness to please."

"And you're pointing this out because…?"

"Thought you'd want to know—I like being taken advantage of." He left her in her hard plastic chair and crossed to the information desk just down the hall.

He was back in no time, shaking his head as he took the seat next to her. "Nothing yet. She said it shouldn't be much longer."

"Isn't that what they said more than an hour ago?"

"Yeah," he said. "I wanted to ask, I mean, I've been curious."

"About what?"

"About what you see and hear now that you don't have LaShonda in your head."

"So far everything's normal. No ghosts or other spirits. I wonder if I went back to your grandmother's, would I still see her friends?"

"All we have to do is drive out there and find out," he offered. "What are you going to do if you start seeing ghosts of your own?"

"I don't know," she said. "I'll just have to take them as they come. Does the idea bother you?"

"That you might have ghosts hanging around you? Not a bit. Neither will it bother me if you never see another one. Makes no difference to me."

Before long Aaron went again to find out about Mrs. Shelton.

He made three more trips like that throughout the evening before they, along with the police, were allowed to see Mrs. Shelton.

Hailey ignored the cops and their questions, and held Mrs. Shelton's hand to offer the woman, and herself, whatever comfort could be found.

"Mrs. Shelton," Aaron said softly from behind Hailey's shoulder, "what set Charlie off? Why was he so mad today?"

"I lost his key," the woman said.

Hailey leaned forward, knowing this was important. "What key?" she asked.

"That spare key he gave me, the one to the shed."

Chapter 6

One of the cops stepped forward immediately and asked, "What shed?"

Unfortunately, Mrs. Shelton didn't know the answer to that question, and she didn't remember where the key was, either, since Charlie had given it to her five years ago, so they couldn't use it to figure out the location, which Aaron suspected with a sinking feeling was where Charlie kept the kids he stole before he sold them.

With nothing more to be gained from talking to Mrs. Shelton, they heeded the doctor's suggestion that they let her get some rest. The cops went off to lean even harder on Charlie, and Hailey and Aaron went to check on LaShonda one last time for the night.

She was alone in her room, no new roommate

yet, and Aunt Shirley was gone for the night—and she was awake.

"I have to ask, LaShonda," Aaron said, as soon as he could break into the two women's greetings. "Have you remembered anything about the man who took Keenan?"

She rocked her head back and forth on her pillow, then winced at the pain it caused. "No. I knew when he came to the apartment, I'd seen him before, but I can't remember where."

"Okay, that's fine. I'm going to come back tomorrow with a picture for you to—"

"Oh, my God," LaShonda cried, cutting him off. "Look! It's you two, on the news!" She pushed a button in her bed frame and turned up the audio on the TV.

Hailey gasped. "It is."

The 10:00 p.m. newscast was airing a story about Charlie's arrest. Right there on the screen were pictures of Mrs. Shelton, Aaron and Hailey, followed by a shot of Charlie Howard, with a short rundown of his rap sheet.

"That's him!" LaShonda shrieked. "He's the one who took Keenan. Oh, my God! He's the guy from the self-storage place."

"Whoa, back up," Aaron said, his heart going into overdrive. "Where did you say you saw him?"

"The self-storage place. I came out of my unit to get back in the car with Keenan, and he was there. He and Keenan were waving at each other. He was four or five units away."

"What day was this?" Aaron asked.

"It was the day of the tornado. We drove home from there, and the storm hit about an hour later."

"That has to be the shed Mrs. Shelton was talking about," Hailey said to Aaron.

"What are you talking about?" LaShonda demanded. "Do you know where my Keenan is?"

"Not yet," Aaron told her. "Where's this self-storage place?"

The minute she told them, they were out the door. Aaron was on the phone to the cops before they even got to the car.

Because it was after hours when Aaron and Hailey pulled up, the gate was locked, and the place was tightly surrounded in eight-foot-tall chain-link fence, which itself was topped with razor wire.

"Sheesh," Hailey said. "I guess they really don't want anyone to get inside."

"No problem." Aaron drove around the perimeter to the security shack, where he got out of the car to speak with the guard.

Hailey couldn't hear what they said, though she saw Aaron show what she assumed was his D.A.'s office ID, but the guard soon began checking a list and shaking his head.

She got out and joined them. "What's wrong?"

"No listing of Charlie or Charles Howard," Aaron said in disgust. "I knew it was too easy to be true."

"But why would LaShonda have seen him here if he doesn't have a unit here?" Hailey asked.

Aaron shook his head. "She wouldn't. But, hell,

the shed doesn't have to be in his name. In fact, if it was, we would have found it months ago."

"What if it's in his aunt's name?" she asked.

Aaron stared at her for a moment, then grasped her head in his hands and planted a hard kiss on her mouth.

"Shelton," he told the guard. "Wynona Shelton."

"Got her," the guard said.

"Take us there," Aaron demanded.

The guard let them in and took them on his security-company golf cart to the unit in question.

"This is it," he told them.

"Okay, open it up," Aaron said.

"Only the renter of each unit has the key," The guard said. "They have to provide their own locks."

Aaron pinched the bridge of his nose. "Look at it this way. I'm an officer of the court, and I'm sure I heard a sound from inside this unit. Since the man I have reason to believe frequents this unit happens to be awaiting trial for kidnapping and selling children, I don't think I want to wait until we can wake up a judge to get a search warrant. I'm sure I hear someone crying inside this unit. This is what we call exigent circumstances."

Hailey heard the sounds of approaching sirens just as the guard pulled a pair of bolt cutters from beneath his seat.

"Let's use my master key," the guard said.

In less than a minute, they were inside the unit and had the light on.

Hailey leaned around the edge of the door to find three sets of terrified young eyes peeking back from behind a row of boxes. "Oh, my God," she breathed, seeing the three boys cowering in fear.

Aaron stepped inside and spoke quietly. "Hello, boys. You're safe now. I'm Aaron, and this is Hailey. We've come to take you back to your parents."

One of the boys sniffed. "They don't want us anymore."

Aaron squatted down in front of them. "Who told you that?"

"The man."

"The man who brought you here?"

"We're not supposed to talk to strangers," another boy said.

"That's good advice. But it's okay if you talk to me, because I work with the police. And you know what? I think I hear them coming now. Why don't you talk to Hailey while I go meet them?"

While he did that, Hailey stepped inside. There he was. LaShonda's baby.

"You're Keenan," she said softly, hunkering down right in front of him.

His eyes widened. "How did you know that?"

"Because your mother told me." She decided to prepare the boy for what was coming so he wouldn't be shocked or scared when he saw his mother. "She would have come for you herself, but the man who brought you here hurt her, and she's in the hospital. She asked us to find you and bring you to her."

The four-year-old used his fists to rub his eyes. "You mean she didn't give me away?"

"Oh, honey, no. Your mama loves you very much and can't wait to see you again. Will you introduce me to your friends, so we can find their families?"

The next hours were total chaos, with cops and EMTs and reporters overrunning the self-storage grounds.

It was only a few hours until sunrise when Hailey leaned close to LaShonda's bed and woke her. "Hey, girlfriend, wake up, I've got a surprise for you."

LaShonda groaned. "Your name better be Ed McMahon."

Hailey chuckled. "Nope. Come on, wake up. This is better than that. We brought you a visitor."

"Mama?"

"Oh! Keenan? Baby?"

Hailey stepped back out of the way and helped Keenan scoot up onto the bed at his mother's side.

Hailey knew that eventually LaShonda would have dozens of questions, but for now she needed only to hold her son and reassure herself that he was alive and safe.

She backed out of the room and straight into Aaron's arms. He pressed himself against her back and held her close while they peered through the open door at the mother-and-son reunion.

After a few minutes, she turned into his arms and pressed her face against the warmth of his neck.

"Are you crying?" he asked.

She sniffed. "Only a little, the good kind of crying."

"It's okay to feel good. We did a really good thing tonight."

She sniffed and smiled. "I know. You were great tonight."

"So were you."

"We were a good pair, huh?"

"Are," he said. "We *are* a good pair."

Hailey smiled. "You'll get no argument from me."

Chapter 7

"It'll be a miracle if I can stay awake for the ride home," Hailey said when they got to his car.

In the end, she didn't make it. She couldn't remember when she fell asleep, but when she woke, they were parked in front of her building.

She rolled her head against the headrest until she could look him in the eye. "I want, very much, to be brave and bold and sexy and invite you to come up with me."

"Why do I hear a *but* coming next?"

"But I'm about to fall asleep, and you'll be insulted. Besides, I'm still a little shaky from tonight. The only knives I'm used to seeing are of the dinner, steak and butter varieties. And then finding those kids…"

Aaron reached for her hand and held it. "How about if I hold you until you fall asleep?"

Hailey nearly collapsed, she was so grateful for his offer. "You would do that?"

"In a heartbeat. As long as you won't get mad if I fall asleep next to you. I'm still a little shaky myself, after walking into that house and seeing you fighting the sleazeball I've been after for weeks, blood everywhere. I could have lost you today. I could use a little recovery time myself."

If she hadn't have been strapped into her seat, Hailey would have thrown herself into his arms. Getting unstrapped was simple enough. But she saved throwing herself at him for later. Instead, she got slowly out of the car and led him up to her apartment, where she closed the door, sealing them in, shutting the world out.

"I don't mean to sound trite," she told him, "but I don't usually do this sort of thing."

"You mean sleep with a man?"

It was all she could do to keep from stuttering. "What?"

"That's all we're talking about, Hailey. Sleeping. Right?"

She had to clear her throat before she could speak. "Right." She was more nervous now than when she had stared down the creep with the knife. "Right. Maybe this wasn't such a good idea."

Aaron felt her slipping away from him. He didn't want her to slip away. He wanted to hold her, to prove to himself that she was safe and would stay safe at least for tonight.

"Come on," he said. "Let's get you into your bed. Or do you want something to eat first? We should have stopped and had an early breakfast on the way."

"You're hungry?" she asked, relief in her eyes.

Damn, she really was nervous, if mention of food could make her look as if her execution had been postponed.

"I've got frozen pizza," she offered.

"That sounds better than breakfast."

While the pizza heated, Hailey took a shower and changed clothes, since her others had been torn and bloody.

They shared their pizza on the sofa, watching television and catching sight of themselves again on the morning news, which this time also reported on the rescue of the three boys. By the end of the sportscast, Hailey was curled up at one end of the couch, sound asleep.

Aaron smiled softly. She had worn herself out. Trying to act nonchalant about his being there had done her in. He should leave, but he couldn't bring himself to. If she woke up screaming, or even merely scared, he didn't want her to find herself alone.

He knew she would argue with him, but he felt responsible for her nearly getting killed yesterday. He and the police and the bail bondsman and the court should have had Charlie Howard behind bars. If they had, Mrs. Shelton would be home and uninjured. And those three boys would never have gone missing.

He couldn't leave her alone now with her fear.

Gently, he scooped her up in his arms and carried

her to bed. She never woke when he took off her shoes. He left the rest of her clothes on, as well as her bedside lamp.

She looked so damn sweet. The scrapes and bruises she'd suffered earlier made her look vulnerable, but he knew she wasn't. She'd dealt with lightning, ghosts and LaShonda in her head. But not until she'd had to literally fight for her life against an armed man had she shown any fear, and even then, only after the fact.

No, he couldn't leave her. Instead, he slid onto the bed, curled up at her back and wrapped his arms around her.

It was a small, quiet snore that woke Hailey. The way her love life had been going lately, the only sound in her bedroom should have been the alarm clock. Yet she didn't even have time to stiffen before she recognized the heat that snuggled against her back.

The snore was Aaron's.

She smiled. He'd promised to stay until she fell asleep. Apparently he'd been as tired as she had and *had* fallen asleep as he'd suggested he might.

"You're smiling."

"You fell asleep," she said, twisting around until she faced him.

"I did not."

"You snored."

He traced his thumb up and down her arm. "I did not."

"How would you know?" she protested, laughing, shivering from his touch. "You were asleep."

"I see your point."

She followed his suggestive gaze to find her nipples hard and pointing. Heat stung her cheeks. The sweater she'd put on after her shower was thin, and even with her bra covering her beneath it, there was still no mistaking her protruding nipple.

"What are you thinking of?" he asked.

"Lightning."

Her voice was soft and breathy. Aaron was drawn to her the way he had never been drawn to a woman before. He leaned forward and brushed his lips across hers.

"Now," he said, dragging his mouth to a sweet, sweet spot beneath her ear, "is the time for you to tell me to leave."

She arched her neck to give him better access. "Why?"

"Because I'm not going to be able to stop on my own."

She swallowed. "Why would you want to stop?"

Aaron pulled his head away until he could see her eyes. "We're not talking about sleeping this time. We're talking about sex. About making love."

"Oh, I hope so." She slid her arms around his chest and took his mouth with hers. She didn't know where such forwardness came from, she was only grateful she'd found it. She wanted him. She poured herself into the kiss.

A moment later they backed away from each other long enough for her clothes and his to fall away and land on the floor as if by magic. Then they were together again, bare torso to bare torso, breaths comingling, hearts pounding.

For a woman who prided herself on her independence, Hailey gave herself fast to his heat and his strength. After donning a condom from his wallet, he settled himself between her thighs, and she instinctively knew he would give her pleasure the way no other man before him had. He tested and found her ready, then began to enter her.

"Oh, yes," she breathed.

Aaron couldn't speak. She was everything he'd ever wanted in a woman. He might never get enough of her. Then he was there, fully seated. Easing in, then out, back, then forth. Slowly, then slower. Then slow was not enough to feed the hunger inside him. Fire stoked where their bodies were joined and every place she touched him with her soft, delicate hands.

She was with him. He could feel her quivering beneath his weight. Then suddenly she threw her head back and arched her back. A tiny, heart-wrenching scream escaped her throat.

Someone might have said he growled. He couldn't remember one way or the other. All he remembered was flying off the edge of the earth with Hailey in his arms.

He felt as if they'd both been struck by lightning.

Hailey didn't know how long it took her to regain her breath, but when she realized she was finally breathing normally, she felt…reborn. Each breath she took tasted sweeter than any before, regardless of Aaron's weight, which, since he was lying completely atop her, should have been crushing her but instead made her feel safe and cared for. And aroused. Again.

If she felt what she thought she felt against her leg, she wasn't the only one who was already aroused again. She smiled.

Aaron pushed himself up on his forearms. "You look pretty pleased with yourself."

"I'm pretty pleased with you, me and the whole wide world right now."

He nudged his nose against hers and trailed his lips across her cheeks. "Sounds like a sentiment I can endorse."

"I was hoping you'd say that." She reached over and pulled open the drawer of her nightstand. She pulled out a box of condoms and placed it next to the lamp.

The next hours proved to be unlike any Hailey could have imagined. They made love in the bed twice, and then in the shower. They might have gone another round, but then they realized that would mean another shower, which would mean showering together. Since he had to go to the office, they were going to have to stop making love.

"For now," they both agreed.

"Remind me when I go see Mrs. Shelton again to thank her. If it wasn't for her I might never have seen this, um, side of you."

"Oh, yes, you would have." He sidled up to her until his towel pressed against hers. He slipped his arms around her and pulled her to his damp chest. "I like to think that we would have found each other one way or another, you and I."

"I'm glad you feel that way." She flattened her hand against his chest. "I need to be completely honest with you before anything between us goes any further."

"This sounds serious." Aaron pressed a fingertip to the pulse at the base of her throat. "Your heart's pounding."

She nodded. "I guess it is, but…what I'm going to say doesn't have to be a big deal unless you want it to be. I'm just telling you so you'll know before we spend any more time together. Sometime between your grandmother's pork chops and the snore that woke me up a little while ago, I managed to go and fall in love with you."

"Oh, yeah?" He draped his arms over her shoulders.

"I don't expect you to say anything about it," she said. "I just wanted you to know, that's all."

"You lay yourself open like that and don't expect me to say anything? What if I want to say something?"

She shook her head. "We barely know each other. It's too soon. I'm out of my mind. I shouldn't have said anything."

"So you're taking it back?"

"Are you trying to make me crazy?" she asked. "No, I'm not taking back anything."

"So you still love me?"

"Of course I do."

"So it's not too soon for you to love me, but it is too soon for me to return the feeling?"

"No, that's not what I meant."

"Good." He leaned down and kissed her, softly at

first, then deeper. "Because I do." He kissed her again. "Return the feeling."

He pressed his lips gently to hers again. "I love you, too. How could I not?"

SEEING RED
Debra Cowan

Dear Reader,

While reading stories written by people who had nearly died, I wondered if there were others who had experienced full death and then come back. People who suffered no visible ill effects after too many minutes of being without a pulse and oxygen to the brain. People who regained their ability to function normally...except for one thing.

Firefighter Cass Hollister finds out what happens next after surviving what should've been a fatal fire. She begins to experience bizarre, startling episodes in which she sees full-blown images of fires that haven't happened yet. Fires that could be the work of the vengeful, ex-con brother she sent to prison for arson. Fires she must report to Ben Wyrick, the sexy fire investigator she walked away from months ago.

Now, to catch a deadly arsonist, Cass and Ben will have to trust each other and believe in the visions neither of them can explain.

Dying could be the worst thing that's ever happened to Cass. Or the best. I hope you enjoy finding out.

Warmly,

Debra Cowan

To Sharon Sala, for inviting me to join this anthology. Thanks for your friendship and constant support through the years (and the massage therapist you've been known to share on occasion).

Chapter 1

Cass Hollister's problems began the day she died.

One minute she was pinned beneath a burning beam, flames tearing at her flesh like teeth. The next, she lay on a gurney in the emergency room of a nearby hospital.

Eyes wide, she stared through a gloomy fog at the white acoustical tile ceiling. She tried to blink or respond in some way as a sea of medical personnel flew around her in controlled chaos.

A gray-haired nurse leaned over Cass, checking the IV line already inserted and adjusting the bag of fluids. "CPR isn't working! No pulse, Doctor!"

A young black man worked frantically over her. "Give me one milligram epi!"

Epinephrine? Why? Her heart didn't need to be

restarted. She tried to tell them she wasn't dead, but they couldn't hear her.

She felt herself being sucked into a chilling blackness that slowly squeezed the life out of her. Her entire body went flat like a piece of cardboard, no energy, no pain— nothing.

A wave of electricity ripped through her. The lights began to strobe. Suddenly she felt herself being snapped back and forth through a tight blistering space.

She was back at the fire. Moving through the flames, trying to help a fellow firefighter in trouble. Just as she reached him, a gust of searing air whooshed past her. A scalding solid weight hit her in the back, slamming her face-first into the floor.

Pinned across her back and legs by a beam, she couldn't move as sparks rained down on her, gnawing at exposed flesh.

Her teeth snapped together as she was jerked through another narrow space, then into a dense lifeless sphere.

She was trapped! Why didn't someone help her?

Cass heard someone say, "You have to call it, Dr. Hill."

She was back in the E.R., staring into the physician's dark determined features. He shook his head, filled a syringe and plunged it into her chest.

Crushing pressure bore down on her, and she felt as if a piece of her was breaking off. There was no pain, just a gaping hole.

"She's gone, Doctor. You've done all you can."

I'm not gone! I can hear you! The words wouldn't come.

Cass was dragged down into a spinning vortex of frenzied energy and dropped next to her father, who lay in his casket wearing his dress uniform.

A shrill buzzing sounded in her ears, followed by absolute quiet. Tentacles of smoke wrapped around her, cutting off her air. Suffocating, she tried to fight.

Suddenly a sharp biting acid boiled up her throat. She choked, struggling to claw her way out of the writhing smoke, fighting for oxygen. Finally clean air flowed in. She coughed sharply. Her esophagus felt lacerated.

Someone adjusted the air mask over her nose and mouth, urging her to keep breathing. She blinked up into several disbelieving faces.

"Let's put her on a mechanical ventilator," the young doctor said quietly. "Did someone notify her emergency contact? Decisions will need to be made about the extent of her care."

"I can make them." Cass's voice was muffled behind the oxygen mask.

The people above her started violently, giving a collective gasp.

"Land's sake," breathed a nurse close to Cass.

Looking stunned, the doctor lifted the air mask. "Do you know your name?"

"Cass Hollister." Her throat was raw; her lungs burned. She was suffering from smoke inhalation. Not unusual after fighting a fire, so why were they looking at her so strangely?

The doctor lifted her eyelids and shone his penlight into her eyes. "Today's date?"

She told him.

"Do you remember what happened?"

"We were fighting a fire. A beam fell on me."

"This is incredible," he murmured. "Unheard of."

Things registered for Cass in random order. She smelled like smoke. His name tag read Dr. Hill. Her wrists were burned. "I've been treated for smoke inhalation before, Doc."

"This isn't only smoke inhalation." The man's expression went from shock to amazement. "You had no heartbeat for eleven minutes, Miss Hollister. And no oxygen to your brain."

"Eleven—" Cass's mind whirled. "That's…"

"You flatlined," the doctor said gently. "By every measure we have, you were dead."

Cass gave a choked laugh. "That's impossible."

Dr. Hill shook his head. "I would agree—except that we witnessed it."

Her throat, already sore from smoke, went tight. "Dead as in *dead?*"

Panic and inexplicable dread unfurled inside her. She fought to remain calm. She was probably pumped full of some drug, and it was playing with her mind.

He nodded, watching her as if he expected her to pass out any minute. "You came in with severe hypoxia. No oxygen to the brain. That caused an elevated heart rate, but your heart couldn't keep that up, so it stopped pumping."

She heard him, but the words seemed to come from far away.

Her head throbbed sharply. Smoke headache, not uncommon after fighting a fire. Although she hadn't felt this strange sense of floating after fighting other fires.

The doctor was talking about running tests for brain damage, but all Cass could think was *dead*. She'd been dead.

Maybe that explained the weird sense of being yanked through space. Had she had a near-death experience? Did people really have those?

The pain in her throat should have been excruciating, but it wasn't. Another strange thing. A sense of euphoria swelled inside her, followed by a hollowed-out feeling of sadness.

When Dr. Hill said he would update her captain, she nodded absently.

Dead. Was that why she'd seen her father? Mike Hollister had been gone six years. Six long years in which she'd followed in his footsteps as an Oklahoma City firefighter and tried to make him proud. Six years in which her twin brother, Lee, had landed himself in prison for arson.

He hated their father. He hated Cass.

Dr. Hill removed the air mask and asked her to breathe. When she did, his jaw dropped. "You shouldn't be breathing on your own yet. Of course, you shouldn't be doing any of this."

Her heart had stopped. She'd died. Overwhelmed by emotion, she grabbed his hand. "Thank you."

He squeezed her hand in return, smiling. "There are some questions I want to ask, but a fire department investigator has been waiting to talk to you. If you're not up to it, I'll tell him to come back later."

"I'm up to it."

"That's good," a man said in a quiet baritone from the doorway.

Sensation broke through her hard shell of numbness. A shiver stroked up her spine. Only one voice had ever melted her from the inside out.

The brawny black-haired man stepped into view, and Cass's heart took a tumble. Ben Wyrick.

Maybe she really *was* dead, and this was hell.

She'd nearly died. In fact, according to everything the nurse had told him, she *had* died. He didn't want to admit how hard the news had hit him.

It had been eight months since that night at his house when Cass had told him they were over. The sight of her, the memory of her silky skin, made his pulse hitch, but it was her pale, soot-streaked face and the emotion swimming in her eyes that shook something loose inside him. Being this close to her brought on a tide of emotions, ranging from anger to relief.

It wouldn't matter if eight months passed or eight decades. Ben didn't think he would ever be able to look at her without wanting to touch her. It was more than the way she looked. There was a sweetness about her, a warmth.

Her thick shoulder-length hair, the color of spiced tea, was in its usual neatly twisted braid. French braid, she'd told him once.

She wore a pale blue hospital gown, her breasts full and loose beneath the fabric. Her boots and navy pants sat neatly under the gurney.

The raw burns on her wrists looked tender and

sent anger sweeping through him. Right now, she was staring at him with those dusky green eyes, and they shut off his brain for just a moment, just as they had the first time he'd met her. Thumping himself mentally, he rubbed his nape. "How're you feeling?"

"Like I swallowed fire," she said hoarsely.

The deep dimple to the left of her mouth flashed, then was gone, but it was enough to make his body go tight.

For the fiftieth time, he wished he didn't have to see her, but thanks to training classes, vacations and illness, the other fire investigators were unavailable. And he'd cussed about that the whole way to the hospital. Admittedly, part of him had wanted to reassure himself that she was okay. She was and he had, but he couldn't leave.

"Is it okay to talk now? How's your throat?"

"It's a little uncomfortable, but nothing like what I've felt before." She gave a wan smile, brushing her bangs away from her eyes.

The gesture reminded him of the first time he'd seen her hair down. It had also been the first time they'd slept together. Images of the thick ginger-colored silk against his belly, sliding through his hands, flooded his mind.

Her appeal wasn't only physical. She had more integrity than almost anyone he knew, and it had cost her dearly when she'd testified against her brother for arson.

Hell. He needed to do his job and get out. "Can you walk me through what happened?"

She recapped the sequence of events after her

arrival at the downtown hotel, which was in the midst of being renovated. Despite having eaten a massive quantity of smoke, her voice hardly sounded hoarse.

"Captain Tenney ordered us out. I was in the rear of the hotel and headed for the nearest exit when I saw another firefighter in one of the offices. His radio wasn't working."

She paused, and Ben looked up from his notes to find her waiting expectantly. He had questions, but he wanted to hear her version of events uninterrupted first. "Go on."

"I went over to lead him out, and the next thing I knew, the beam knocked me flat."

And caused her death. He still couldn't believe it. "Who was it? The other firefighter."

"I don't know. His helmet was pulled down so low, I could barely see his eyes."

"Didn't he have a name on his turnout coat?" The smells of antiseptic and smoke drifted around Ben.

"No, not that I saw, and I didn't see a station number on the side of his helmet, either."

"So you have no idea who it was?"

She shook her head. "Someone else on the crew might."

"I'll be talking to them later. Probably figure it out then."

"You'll let me know what you find out?"

"Sure." He needed to talk to the other firefighters, her captain and the incident commander and get a better picture, but Ben already had a kink in his gut.

It was curious but not impossible that Cass hadn't recognized the firefighter, but he might have been from one of the other station houses that had responded to the alarm. That wasn't what got Ben's attention. What did was the fact that the man had worn no identification, neither station number nor name.

The woman in front of him still brought out his primitive instinct to protect. He wanted to touch her so he could feel for himself that she was okay. But he didn't need to do that. And he sure as hell *shouldn't* do it.

She wasn't interested in a relationship. That was what she'd told him. The thought that she was probably already seeing someone else had his jaw clamping tight enough to shatter his teeth.

He wasn't going to ask. It had nothing to do with the case, but his next question did. He had no evidence to support his suspicion, but he couldn't dismiss the possibility that a too-familiar arsonist might be involved.

"I heard Lee was out."

Guilt and sadness crossed her face. "I heard that, too."

"Has he contacted you?"

"C'mon, Ben. You know he hates my guts."

"I thought he might've gotten in touch with you just to rub it in that he's free."

Three years ago, Cass had caught her twin in the act of arson and provided the testimony that sent him to prison. She'd become something of a legend after that.

From Ben's short time with her, he knew she had tried to keep in touch with her brother, but after being rejected constantly when she visited him in prison, she'd finally let it go.

"His parole officer contacted me the second day Lee was out, saying he hadn't checked in. I doubt he has since—or will."

"I imagine you're right. I'm going to ask around, see if I can get a lead on where he might be. Just to rule him out."

"Good idea." Fatigue shadowed her eyes. "If I hear anything, I'll pass it on."

"Okay." He had enough from her for now, so he should get out of here. The longer he stayed, the closer the walls seemed to get. She didn't exactly look comfortable with his presence, either. "If I have more questions, I'll be in touch."

Something flashed in her eyes—longing?—then disappeared. "Okay."

He turned to go. "I'm glad you're all right."

"Thanks."

He nodded, wishing he didn't feel the need to escape, especially since he didn't have the option of keeping his distance from her, at least not until he figured out what had started the blaze at the hotel.

Why had Cass been the only one hurt? From her description of what had happened, and the pictures he'd taken, that beam shouldn't have been loosened by the part of the roof that had collapsed.

Looking at her pale face made Ben furious that this had happened to her. And it made him feel, he had to admit, furious at *her*. He'd been kidding himself to think he could see her and not feel anger. Or the heavy throb of desire. He wanted her. He would probably always want her. But he wasn't going to do anything about it.

Thinking about how she'd walked away should've cooled his blood, but it didn't. He'd finally gotten her out of his head. And seeing her just now had put her right back in.

Despite trying not to, Cass was still thinking about Ben hours later as she lay in the darkness, listening to the softly humming monitors hooked up to her head and chest. Moonlight lapped like water against the floor each time the air from the vent fluttered the thin curtains.

After Ben left, the doctor had moved her to a permanent room, saying she had to stay at least overnight for observation.

Seeing Ben had filled her with regret. She still believed she'd made the right decision to end their relationship, but she'd handled it poorly. He was better off without her.

His presence had caused a swell of longing inside her. It had also set off the awareness that skimmed the surface of her skin whenever he was near. He was a big man. Shoulders as wide as a door, strong neck, brawny chest covered with hair as black as that on his head. He was a wall of hard striated muscle.

His deep blue eyes were intense, perfect for the unpolished bluntness of his features. Her dad would've said Ben's face had character. His nose was slightly crooked. Deep laugh lines bracketed his mouth, and the dark shadow of a beard was always there on his sun-weathered skin. His hands were big, too, callused, with long fingers. And incredibly gentle.

His appearance might've been too bold for some, but not for her. She'd been drawn to everything about him. After not seeing him for so long, that realization had barreled over her the instant he'd stepped into the E.R.

His manner had been distant yet polite. After what she'd done, that was probably more than she should have expected.

Her wrists were stiff with gauze, but at least the earlier pain had dimmed to a throbbing ache. She still felt detached, empty. As if there was no substance to her body. Except for when Ben had been here, and then everything inside her had come alive.

She didn't want to go to sleep. Not only because she was afraid she might dream about him, but also because she was afraid she might not wake up. Still, the strain was too much. She tried to stay awake but felt herself drifting off.

She knew it was a dream as soon as it started. She was on duty in a well-known department store that was rapidly being engulfed by a blaze. Somewhere a child wailed. Moving as quickly as possible, she followed the sound to the back of the store. No one was there.

She heard her captain's order to evacuate, and she turned to leave. Eruptions of heat and sparks and fire boiled around her, beneath her, snatching her down into a quicksand of hell.

Blinding gray smoke obliterated her flashlight beam. Someone grabbed her ankle, and she reached down to help them. Instead of a person, she gripped a ball of flame, a living incinerator that writhed around her hands like vines.

Her flesh burned as if bare. Where were her gloves? Frantic, she tried to beat off the flames ripping at her hands.

It was too late. The fire peeled off the first layer of her skin, chewing through the flesh, searing her nerve endings.

She shot bolt upright in bed, gasping for air as a cold sweat slicked her spine. Unbearable agony drew her hands into cramped, closed fists. Something was wrong. She needed light.

Flipping the switch was excruciating. She turned her hands over and cried out. Blisters covered her palms. Blood-red bubbles of skin from the bases of both palms to the tips of her fingers.

Tears blurred her vision. She dried her eyes on the sheet and looked again.

A dizzying heat washed over her as she stared at her palms, then touched them. Only smooth flesh, undamaged by fire. There were no blisters. None.

Chapter 2

If there were any reason that would make Ben even less eager to see Cass than he had been yesterday, this was it.

The answers he'd gotten from the other firefighters at the scene were forming a picture that hollowed out his gut. So far, everything he'd found pointed to Cass's "accident" as being a premeditated act.

By the time he had seen her at the hospital the first time, it was three in the morning. The hours since then had been spent at the scene or interviewing witnesses well into the afternoon. After grabbing a sandwich for supper, he returned to the hospital.

His eyes were gritty from fatigue, and he needed sleep, but he knew he needed to talk to Cass first.

The door to her private room was open, and he

paused outside. Flowers and balloons crowding the wall-length windowsill made the space look and smell like a flower shop. He rapped on the door. "Hello?"

"Ben? Come in." She barely sounded hoarse today.

He stepped inside and found her sitting up in bed, wrists still bandaged. Her thick hair was down, sliding around her shoulders in a silky cloud.

Not wanting anyone else to hear what he had to say, he closed the door. He caught a whiff of soap and shampoo, and was unable to tear his gaze from the heavy satin of Cass's hair. He wanted to bury his hands in it, his face. Cutting off those thoughts, he shifted his attention to her.

"How are you feeling today?"

"Not too badly. My throat hardly even hurts. The burns are healing quickly." She glanced at her hands, then curled them into fists, a strange look crossing her face. "The nurse helped me wash my hair and take a bath. It's good to get rid of the smoke smell."

Her clean fresh scent teased him as he took in the dewy skin of her face and neck. Instead of a hospital gown, she wore her own sleepwear—a red tank top that hinted at her deep cleavage, and he knew that, under the sheet, she had on the matching polka-dotted red shorts. She cleared her throat, and he realized he was staring.

Jaw tight, he forced his attention to her face. He wasn't the only one affected, he realized, as he caught the awareness shimmering in her eyes.

She lifted her chin. "The doctor said I can go home in the morning, but I have to come back for a check-up in a week."

Ben dragged a hand across his sweat-dampened nape, determined to channel his thoughts back to the case. "That's great. Still pretty unbelievable, but great. You're lucky."

"This whole thing has been so bizarre," she murmured.

"Yeah." Standing at the foot of her bed, he suddenly became aware of the dirt and ash on his jeans and navy OCFD T-shirt. He should've showered and changed before coming here, but his suspicions were so strong that he had cared only about getting to Cass. "There are some things I need to touch base with you about."

"Did you find out about that firefighter? Who he is?"

"I still don't know. None of the other firefighters or the incident commander saw the guy."

"You mean I was the only one?"

"Yeah."

She stared down at her clasped hands, brushing her thumb back and forth across the opposite palm. "Maybe I hallucinated him."

"Are you saying you're unsure now of what you saw?" If she were, it could be a result of her dead-but-not-dead experience. "Cass?"

"I'd just hoped someone else might have seen him." She rubbed at her palms again. "It's just that I wouldn't blame you if you didn't trust me."

"What happened between us doesn't have anything to do with this fire," he said stiffly. "It's in the past. Leave it there."

Her mouth tightened. "All right."

He felt like hitting something. Why did she have

to bring up their past? It had no relevance here. He wouldn't let it. "I found a length of rope near where you fell. Do you remember seeing it?"

"No. Do you think it had something to do with my accident?"

"It was tied to the beam that fell on you, and the construction foreman hadn't seen it before. He said there was no reason for it to be there."

"That's strange. I don't get it."

He might as well tell her all of it at once. "The beam that fell on you was cut."

Apprehension crossed her face.

As matter-of-factly as he could, Ben continued. "The reason that beam fell on you wasn't because it was weakened in the fire. It was because someone cut a notch in it and pulled it down with the rope."

She blinked. "To deliberately hurt someone?"

"Not someone," he said grimly. "*You.*"

The color drained out of her face. "Why would someone want to hurt me?"

She had to be thinking about her brother. Ben sure was. "We need to figure that out. You're sure this mystery fireman motioned you over?"

"Yes."

"Is that an area you would've gone to if he hadn't?"

Massaging her hands, she shook her head. "No. Those offices had already been checked and cleared. We were ordered out."

Dread snarled Ben's gut.

Her troubled gaze pinned his. "So that fire was arson."

He hated that she was coming to the same conclusion he had. "Matchbook and paper starter. Most likely the arsonist set the fire, then waited, wearing firefighter gear, for y'all to arrive on the scene."

She looked horrified. "He was waiting for *me*?"

"It appears that way. Your name is on your turnout coat, so it wouldn't have been hard for him to blend in and keep track of you."

"Whoever it was could've found out my schedule and set the fire knowing I'd respond to the call."

He nodded, concern mixing with anger.

"Lee could've found that out," she whispered.

Ben's jaw locked. He wanted to stop whoever was doing this, not only because it was his job, but also because Cass was the one being threatened.

"No one else saw him." Horror crept into her voice as realization set in. "He made that beam fall on me."

"I have no proof it's your brother."

"It is. I know it." Tears filled her eyes.

Everything inside him urged him to hold her, but he knew how stupid—and unwelcome—that would be.

"Is there anyone else who might want to hurt you?"

"I hope not. I don't think so."

"Has anything strange happened in the last few months?"

"You mean besides that whole freaky thing yesterday when I came back to life? No."

"No one's threatened you at a scene? No trouble at work?"

"No."

"What about dating?"

Her eyes widened. "What does that have to do with anything?"

"Maybe nothing." He wanted to know, that's what, but the truth was that it also might matter. "Have you been seeing anyone? Had a bad breakup?" Thanks to their history, he knew that was a definite possibility.

"I haven't been seeing anyone. Not since… No."

"Anyone asking you out who won't take no for an answer?"

"Nothing like that."

Ben told himself the reason he was relieved was because it narrowed his suspect list, but that was a lie. He was glad she hadn't drop-kicked him and immediately hooked up with someone else. Which meant he was letting things get too personal.

His shoulders went tight. "I talked to Lee's parole officer again on the way over, and he's heard nothing. There's a warrant out to pick up your brother, but he's still MIA. When you get out of here, you can't go home."

"Where am I supposed to go?"

Ben noticed she kept rubbing her hands nervously. No wonder. Someone had tried to kill her. He wanted to be the one to protect her, but he couldn't be. He wasn't going to let himself cross a line he might not be able to recross. Things between them had to stay professional.

"For a while, you'll need to stay somewhere besides your house. What about with friends? Maybe Jana and Tim Daniels?"

"No. Lee knows them. If I stay there, there's a chance they could be hurt. I don't want that."

"Okay." He would feel the same in her place, but he didn't know an alternative.

She was silent for so long that his mind started working in a direction he didn't like. He could stay with his brother until this was over, and Cass could stay at *his* place.

He didn't want that. She was already in his head; he didn't need her flirty scent in every inch of his house.

"I can stay at the firehouse," she said. "It won't matter that I'm not cleared to work."

"That's a good idea." Both disappointment and relief charged through him. The fire station was manned 24/7. No one could walk in or out without being noticed. "I'll talk to your captain, too. I want him to be aware there's a threat."

She massaged her hands again.

"Your hands okay? Should I get a nurse?"

"No, they're fine." She shoved them beneath the sheet. "Do I have to go into hiding?"

"No, but if you need to go somewhere, don't go alone. I'm not the only one looking for Lee, so we'll find him. It just may take a while."

The anxiety in her eyes hit him hard. Even though her staying at the firehouse was the best solution, it didn't feel like the *right* one. Even so, he refused to let this be about anything except the job.

He'd ridden in that rodeo before. More than once, since their breakup, he'd been glad he hadn't asked her what he'd originally planned the night everything fell apart between them. Not to move in with him, but to marry him.

As it was, she hadn't been able to get away from him fast enough.

Yeah, he was keeping as much distance from Cass as possible.

He wasn't going to let her get hurt, but he also wasn't going to let her hurt *him* again.

Ben's visit was still fresh in Cass's mind the next day. Someone had tried to kill her, and her brother was a likely suspect. And if that weren't enough to have her reeling, there was her reaction to Ben to contend with. Just because he still got to her, that didn't mean she'd been wrong to leave him.

Tension whipped her nerves taut. She was glad to be out of the hospital, although she wished she were home. Unable to return there at all, she had asked Jana to bring some clothes and toiletries to the firehouse. She wished she were staying with Ben, but it was better that distance remain between them. Being around him could make her second guess her decision about breaking things off.

She still wanted him. She couldn't call her body's reaction to him anything *except* want. The way he'd looked at her in the hospital had put her hormones on simmer. Her pulse hitched as she remembered the undisguised desire in his eyes.

Did he feel anything except lust for her now? If so, she couldn't tell.

As she finished the kitchen cleanup for the guys who'd answered a call, the television blaring, a local news anchor broke into the programming to report an arson fire at Mercer's department store. The blaze had claimed the life of a child. Every detail slammed into Cass like a two-by-four.

Everything was exactly as she'd dreamed last night.

Sweat broke out over her whole body. She sank into the nearest chair and put her head between her knees to keep from throwing up.

Her stomach began to cramp as a theory formed. The vision of that fire had happened after she'd died and been resuscitated. It had to be related to that.

Could this be possible? Had she really seen a fire before it happened?

Cass told herself that seeing the department store fire before it happened was a fluke. But when she saw another arson fire the next morning—this time without falling asleep first—and learned hours later that it, too, had happened, she called Ben and asked him to come to the firehouse. She didn't want to, but she had to.

As they sat in his white SUV, night settled over the city in sooty layers. It was too hot to talk outside, and she didn't want to discuss this in front of her fellow firefighters. Ben's vehicle was the best place for their conversation.

Cold air blasted from the vents. He angled his broad shoulders into the corner and draped one big hand over the steering wheel.

The sleeves of his white dress shirt were rolled back to reveal strong forearms. Crisp black hair showed in the vee left by two open shirt buttons, and he wore navy slacks. Typically, he wore a suit only when testifying in court.

He shoved a hand through his short dark hair, the fabric of his shirt pulling taut across his muscular upper arm. Dark blue eyes zeroed in on her. "You sounded shaky on the phone. You okay?"

"Yes." *For a freak.*

His eyes glittered like dark glass in the shadows. Her gaze slid over his corded neck, the strong line of his throat. She was hit with the urge to put her mouth there. Kiss him. Lick him. Like that would ever happen again.

Quietly he said, "You don't look like you've gotten much sleep since leaving the hospital."

"I haven't." *And you're getting ready to find out why.* She took a deep breath. There was no good way to do this. "Let me get all this out before you say anything, okay?"

Eyes narrowing, he hesitated then nodded.

"I was… After I…" she began haltingly. How did you tell someone who dealt in hard evidence that you saw fires before they happened?

She plunged in. "Since the accident, I've had these…episodes. It's like I'm at a fire. I see the location, the victims…all kinds of details."

She touched her hands, still astonished that there were no blisters there. No way was she telling him about those. She already sounded like a crazy person. "But these aren't dreams. The most recent one happened when I was wide awake. The first one was in the hospital. I saw the fire at Mercer's department store."

Ben straightened, coming to attention at her words.

"At first I thought it was a nightmare. Then I heard

about it on the news. Everything about it was exactly what I saw."

Her voice began to shake. Hearing herself talk about her visions aloud, sharing it with Ben, unsettled her even more. "I didn't know what was happening until I saw the news and realized—" Was she really going to say this out loud?

"Realized what?"

Every doubt, every jeer she'd uttered to herself, was in his tone. "That I'm seeing fires before they happen."

The silence was immediate and heavy with disbelief. Drawing out until her nerves stretched taut. "I know it sounds like voodoo witchy stuff, all right?"

He said softly, "It sounds like post-traumatic stress disorder."

"I thought about that, but how could I know details like the specific building or what was inside or the victims if I hadn't really seen those fires?"

"Because of your brother," he said bluntly.

"What about him?" Then she understood. "You think he's the arsonist and he's telling me what he's going to do? You can't be serious!"

"It makes sense."

"No, it doesn't! He hates me. He's not going to confide in me."

"Confide, no. But he might give you the information in order to put you in a bad position, to compromise your job."

Stunned, she stared at him. "Well, he isn't! I just told you how I know about these fires. I don't see who sets them or how they start."

"Okay, when's the next one?"

"What?"

"When's the next fire?" he challenged. "And where?"

"I don't know! This hasn't been happening long enough for me to figure it out. This seems just as weird to me as it does to you, believe me." Probably more so, thanks to the blisters that came and went. She didn't blame him for his doubt, but it irritated her anyway. "All I know is these fires took place hours after I...saw them."

A muscle pulsed in his jaw. "It would be understandable if you wanted to share information about Lee without actually informing on him. I know how you beat yourself up after testifying against him."

"That isn't what's going on." Her voice cracked. How could Ben think she would cover for an arsonist, even her brother? Especially since she'd been the one to turn him in three years ago. "Maybe it *is* him, but I don't *know* that."

"You're telling me everything?"

"Yes," she lied, thinking about the blisters.

Apparently she'd hesitated too long, because he pinned her with those piercing blue eyes. She held his gaze, trying to appear calm even as her heart slammed in her chest. She fought not to blurt out the rest of the story.

His gaze was sharp, ruthless. "What do you think I can do with this information? Am I supposed to wait until you get one of these dreams or visions or whatever they are, then put out a call and ask for extra men to watch whatever place you claim to see?"

"I don't know what you should do." Nerves wound tight, she rubbed at her hands again. They were stiff and sore. "I don't know who it is, and I don't know when the next fire will be! Maybe nearly dying *did* leave me with brain damage, but I thought I should tell you what was happening. I couldn't keep quiet, knowing my information might help prevent a fire or stop one before it kills someone else."

She told herself Ben's skepticism wasn't personal. The story *was* fantastic. It was happening to her, and even she couldn't believe it.

She looked him in the eye. "I wouldn't lie."

"I know that." There was no hesitation, no doubt. "But this is pretty damn hard to believe."

"I'm having a little trouble with that myself." As certain as she was that she was seeing fires beforehand, the knowledge still rattled her. She wanted to throw herself in his arms, but was so shaken by how much she wanted that—and by the whole conversation—she opened the car door to escape. A wave of steamy air hit her face. "Thanks for coming."

Before she could move, her cell phone rang.

It was the groundskeeper at the cemetery where her father was buried.

"What's wrong?" Ben asked when she hung up.

He was the last person she wanted to tell, but she couldn't stop herself. "My father's headstone has been vandalized. I have to go to the cemetery."

"I'll drive you."

"No." She would call Jana or Tim.

As she began to slide out, Ben cupped her elbow. "You aren't supposed to go anywhere alone."

Off balance, she started to argue, but she just didn't have it in her. "Thanks," she said in a half whisper, and pulled the door closed.

Lee resented their father, and this act of vandalism, so close on the heels of the fires, felt to her like further proof that her brother was the arsonist. Her stomach sank.

"I think it's Lee," Ben said.

His hand felt hot on her flesh, but she tried to ignore that as he went on.

"But if it *is* him, and this is his way of telling you he's behind these fires, why not just contact you instead of playing this game?"

"A question I'd like to have answered, too."

He removed his hand and put the SUV in gear. "I'm sorry, Cass. For all of this."

Nodding, she stared out the window.

She wasn't sure what she had expected when she told him, but it hadn't been him accusing her of covering for her brother.

Or him offering to go with her to the cemetery. She shouldn't read anything into that. His presence was for her protection, for the case.

She suddenly, fiercely, wished it were about her.

Chapter 3

Seeing fires before they happened? If Ben didn't know better, he would think Cass was on drugs. Or having an allergic reaction to something they'd given her when she left the hospital.

But she'd never done recreational drugs, and he knew the doctor hadn't prescribed anything, so there was nothing to cause an adverse reaction. Apparently the trauma she'd suffered had affected her more deeply than she'd first let on. Maybe some part of her brain really had been damaged. Regardless, she was upset, so it had seemed only right to insist on driving her to the cemetery.

What did she expect him to do about her claim that she "saw" fires before they happened? What *could* he do? For right now, he would start by not letting her out of his sight.

A fierce sense of protectiveness swept over him, but he dismissed it and told himself that what he felt was responsibility. She was a victim, a witness. Right now, she happened to be part of his job. That didn't mean she was part of his life. He had to be careful not to get sucked in again.

His doubts about her getting information from some kind of vision had nothing to do with the fact she'd dumped him, but with plain old disbelief in that kind of paranormal crap and with her low-life brother being a convicted arsonist. It made sense that Lee Hollister was the torch and tipping Cass off as a means to taunt her. To show her that she couldn't stop him. And in Ben's opinion, her turning Lee in three years ago was reason enough for her not to turn him in again. The whole ordeal had been hell for her.

No matter where Cass got her information, there was no doubt she was certain of it. Just as there was no ignoring the fact that she was afraid. She'd probably expected him not to believe her story, but if what she'd told him could save a life or stop a fire, he couldn't afford to dismiss it.

Though he had no proof, he still suspected Lee was the one who had started the fire and rigged that beam to try to kill his sister. The SOB needed to be sent back to prison for good, before he made another attempt on Cass's life or started more fires, and Ben wanted to be the one to send him on that one-way trip. Right now, the best chance Ben had of finding the bastard was to spend more time with Cass.

It was the best and most logical thing to do. And the worst. Being near her drove him crazy. Her soft floral scent scrambled his thoughts, and he couldn't help remembering the sweetness of that honey-and-cream skin—her neck, her breasts, her thighs. He wanted another taste. *Man, don't go there.* Pure torture.

Once they reached the cemetery, he followed her directions around a curve and parked on the side of the asphalt road. Regularly spaced light poles put off a filmy glow as Ben and Cass passed neatly tended plots. The light swam with shadows, making the ground appear to move, though that wasn't what had the hair on Ben's neck rising.

It was the heavy feel of the night. Silent…still. Threatening. Oklahoma was rarely without wind, and its absence, combined with the steamy temperature, made the air a dead weight. The way it was in the seconds before a tornado.

The groundskeeper was waiting patiently next to Mike Hollister's headstone, aiming his flashlight so the beam fully illuminated the grave marker's stony face.

The rectangular stone, arched at the top and made of gray granite, was all but destroyed. Cass drew a sharp breath. Ben could practically feel the hurt well up inside her. Chunks of rock had been gouged out, leaving holes that gaped like empty eye sockets.

She knelt, touching the damaged facade.

"Looks like someone took a sledgehammer to it," Ben said.

"Dad's name is gone."

The word *Father* had been obliterated, as well. The crime was clearly personal. In Ben's opinion, Lee had to be responsible. Who else had motive? Who else hated the dead man so much?

In the glow of light, with her head bent, Cass looked small, alone. Anger burned inside Ben. When they had been together, she had sometimes talked about her brother's bitterness toward their father, how he'd never had the balls to tell the old man he didn't want to be a smoke eater. Cass had excelled at fighting fires, though, making Mike Hollister proud. And Lee even more resentful.

The groundskeeper said he'd already viewed the security tape, but the cameras hadn't gotten a clear image of the vandal. Even so, he apologized for not catching the culprit.

As the man walked away, Ben thanked him. He expected to hear Cass do the same, but when she said nothing, he looked down at her.

Moonlight limned one side of her body, turning her profile a cool silver. She was staring straight ahead, eerily motionless.

"Cass?"

No answer. She didn't so much as twitch a muscle. It was as if she didn't hear him.

Concerned, he stepped closer. "Cass?"

She gave a keening moan and gripped the headstone, doubling over.

What the hell? Ben lunged, hooking an arm around her waist to catch her before she pitched face-first into the granite.

He fell to his knees, and she sagged into him. "You okay?"

She didn't answer. Beneath his hold, her muscles were locked tight. Her breath sawed in and out of her lungs, and her pulse was hammering so hard in her throat that he could see it even in the dark shadows. There was a sheen of perspiration on the curve of her neck. Ben's heart kicked hard. What was going on? Was she having a seizure? People with head trauma did that sometimes.

Sobbing, she drew back and thrust her hands toward him. "Look! Look at my palms!"

He did. And sucked in a breath that knifed painfully through his lungs. He told himself the light was playing tricks on his eyes. He couldn't be seeing what he thought he was.

"I saw another fire," she whispered.

Ben couldn't look away. Her palms were covered in blisters, open pockets of boiled skin.

What was he seeing? What the hell was going on?

Tears streaming down her face, Cass demanded hoarsely, "Get your cell phone. Quick! Take a picture."

Operating on reflex, barely aware of moving, he whipped the phone out of his pocket, flipped it open and clicked a shot of her palms.

"Another one," she choked out.

He did, then paused. There were no blisters. Thinking there must be a problem with the view-finder, he lowered the phone.

She lifted her hands, palms up. "They're gone."

Gone. Just like that. He stared hard, his brain

numb. Adrenaline shot through him, and he rose, helping her to her feet. "Are you okay? Let me take you to the emergency room."

"I'm fine. I just need a second to get a hold of myself."

"I might need more than a second," he muttered, moving her away from the headstone. He slid an arm around her waist and steered her toward his SUV. "You need to sit."

He wanted to make sure nothing else was wrong with her. He hadn't just seen what he thought he had. He couldn't have.

"I'm fine. Really."

She didn't look fine. She looked afraid, defeated.

He kept his arm around her in case she started to tumble again and he needed to catch her. Hell, someone might need to catch *him*. "You don't seem surprised by what just happened."

"I'm not. It…it happened before, too."

She trembled, and tears ran down her cheeks. Ben didn't know if she was even aware of them. He opened the passenger door and set her carefully on the edge of the seat to face him. "How many of these episodes have you had?"

"Three now."

"You've gotten blisters every time?"

"Yes."

"Are they always this bad?"

"Yes. They haven't gotten worse. I guess that's good."

"Let me see your hands again."

She reluctantly obliged.

Staring at her palms, he shook his head. Her flesh was smooth. There wasn't even a hint of redness. How was this possible? He'd seen those blisters, seen how badly burned her hands had been.

She believed her near-death experience had something to do with these episodes. He couldn't prove differently.

Son of a… Ben felt disoriented, as if he were trying to find his way blindfolded along the edge of a cliff. Something weird was definitely going on, and neither of them could explain it. Maybe there *was* no explanation.

He gently brushed his fingers across one of her palms. "Does this hurt?"

"No." She tugged her hand free of his hold.

Her skin was damp with sweat, and he lifted a hand to push a stray lock of hair away from her face. She stared up at him with those deep green eyes, searching his face. For what? Reassurance, maybe? He didn't have any.

He became aware then of how close together they were standing. Her flirty scent had his nerve endings throbbing. His body went tight.

He wanted to touch her petal-smooth skin, her warmth. He needed to feel her. Comfort her.

Damn, he needed comfort himself.

Her voice cracked. "Lee destroyed Dad's headstone. I know it was him."

The devastation in her face cut Ben deep. He pulled her close and wrapped his arms around her.

Burying her face in his shoulder, she gave a choked sob. Hesitantly, her hands rose to his waist, then slid around to splay across his back as her tears dampened his shirt. She held on, her breasts flattened against him, her head tucked beneath his chin.

Her skin-warmed scent settled in his lungs, chiseled away at his control. He should release her, but he couldn't make himself do it.

After a moment, Cass lifted her head, swiping at her tear-stained face. "Sorry. I lost it there for a second."

"You're entitled," he said gruffly. He forced himself to let go, although he couldn't help touching her cheek as he withdrew.

Looking uncertain, she inched back on the seat. "Do you believe me now? That I'm not getting the information from Lee?"

"Yes." Lee might be the torch, but Ben was sure now that Cass wasn't covering for him. She couldn't have faked what he'd just seen.

"He has to be the one behind everything. I can't believe he hates me this much."

"Neither can I," Ben said grimly. He wanted to get his hands around Lee Hollister's throat and squeeze. Before he registered the thought, the words were out. "I won't let him hurt you."

Surprise flared in her eyes as she nodded. As Ben stared down into her face, he inwardly cursed. He was going to protect her, and somehow he had to do it without getting tangled up with her again.

The return trip was short. She refused to go to the E.R., and Ben admitted there was nothing to show the doctors anyway. He was still stunned over what he'd seen happen to her hands. He wanted to help her, but he didn't know how he could, how *anyone* could.

She sat quietly, gazing out the window as they passed trees and houses and city streets. Light from the streetlamps flashed in and out of the car as they drove. Occasionally she would glance down at her hands, then clasp them together.

"Are you going to file a police report about the headstone?"

"I guess, although I don't know that it will do any good."

He studied her profile. "How do you feel? Headache? Pain anywhere?"

"No."

"Tell me what you saw," he said quietly.

"The fire's at an office complex." Her voice was flat. "A new one, northwest of the city, around MacArthur and Memorial."

He knew the area. "One of the finished ones?"

"It's nearly finished. It's across from the bank that's open for business. The fire originated in a small closet."

"So maybe the construction people left some flammables—paint, cleaner, stuff like that?"

"Maybe." She rubbed at her hands, her voice growing agitated. "I hate this. If I'm going to see these things, why can't I see when they'll happen? Or who's doing them? I have no control over it at all."

"You don't need to know when or who. What you saw is enough for us to do something this time. Since we have no idea when it might happen, we need to make a plan."

She nodded.

"You saw the first fire six hours before it happened, and the second one more than ten."

"Right."

"I can't put a crew on standby for this." He felt, rather than saw, her tense. "But I can do some surveillance on my own."

"Like a stakeout?"

"Yeah."

"That's a good idea." She seemed to relax a bit. "I'm coming, too."

The last thing he wanted was to sit in six feet of space all night with her next to him, smelling her, close enough to touch her, but she was right. She needed to be there. And for all he knew, she might need *him* to be there. What if she had another episode? She shouldn't go through that alone. Besides, the sooner he caught this torch, the quicker he and Cass could go their separate ways.

He pulled up in front of her fire station to let her off. After picking up some things at his office, he would return for her. He asked her to bring her camera for backup pictures and something for them to eat.

"All right." She massaged her hands, and he couldn't help reaching over to cradle them in one of his.

"Do they hurt now?"

"No."

He brushed his thumb across her palm. He still couldn't believe there was no evidence of the blisters that had ravaged her hands. "You rub them a lot. Is it because they're tender?"

"No, they don't feel any different than normal." She tugged her hands from his hold and slid them under her thighs. "I want this to stop."

"Yeah, I imagine you do."

"I'll feel better if we can actually prevent a fire. What if we sit there and nothing happens?"

"We'll consider ourselves lucky."

The sight of her wan features pulled at something inside him. He squeezed her leg. "Don't think about what's bad. Think about what's good. We know the location, thanks to you. If we're there when the fire starts, that gives us a head start on calling dispatch, maybe even stopping it before it starts."

"True." She sounded exhausted.

"Are you sure you're up to this? You've been through a lot. Maybe you should rest."

"A child is dead because of this arsonist. I want to do something. I *need* to."

And this would give her some sense of control.

"Will you have to get approval for the stake-out?" she asked.

"Yeah." She knew he would, so why was she asking? He cocked his head, waiting.

She averted her eyes. "Where will you say you got your information?"

She was afraid he would reveal her secret. "You don't need to worry, Cass. I'll say I got a tip, and if I'm pushed, I'll refuse to disclose my source."

The relief in her face was so great that his chest ached.

Her voice shook. "Thanks for keeping it between us. Of course, no one would believe you if you *did* tell."

He couldn't argue with that. He still wasn't sure he believed it himself.

She made a frustrated sound. "Who gets cursed with stuff like this? Freaks, that's who."

"You're not a freak. I don't understand what's happening, but you're not a freak."

"I want it to stop. Why won't it stop?"

Fear vibrated in every line of her body, and Ben's only thought was to make it go away.

"Hey." He slid his knuckle beneath her chin and turned her face to his. "I know this is scary as hell, but you're going to be able to do something about this fire. That's good."

She didn't look reassured. He smoothed her hair back, grazing his thumb against her cheek. "We'll figure it out."

"You'll help me?" Turmoil darkened her eyes.

He nodded.

"Thank you." Her gaze dropped to his mouth, and danger signals flashed.

When her breath feathered against his lips, he knew she was going to kiss him. And he knew he should stop her.

The first brush of her mouth zinged him to his toes. It was too much. It wasn't enough. He wanted a taste, just one more taste of her.

He settled his mouth on hers and gave in to the hunger that had been building inside him. In an instant, her spicy sweetness, the slick heat of her tongue, overrode every thought. She made a sound in the back of her throat, and whatever restraint he had snapped.

Locking his free arm around her waist, he dragged her closer, cursing the console between them. One soft hand curled around his neck. The full press of her breasts, her soft floral scent, had the blood pounding through him. He took the kiss deeper, urging her into him.

He'd missed her. The way she fit him just right, the teasing stroke of her tongue, the *feel* of her. It took several seconds for him to think past the heated rush of his blood.

Cass was the only woman he'd ever wanted to marry. And he'd been nothing more than a rebound. She hadn't said that, but it was true. The thought penetrated the lust-filled fog in his brain. He remembered the pain. And the anger. They hadn't worked the first time. No reason to think they would now.

He pulled away, breathing hard, his body hurting. "Stop, Cass. Stop."

The dreamy look in her eyes nearly had him saying forget it and pulling her onto his lap. But that would be stupid.

Her mouth was wet from his, and she touched it with trembling fingers. "Ben?"

Her husky voice had his muscles clenching. He started to tell her the kiss meant nothing, but damn it, it *did* mean something.

"That was a bad idea," he said. "We're not going back there."

The pain in her eyes struck hard. He wanted to tell her he didn't mean it, but the truth was, he *had* to mean it.

"You're right." There was a mix of anger and resignation in her voice as she opened her car door. "I'll be ready when you come back."

Ben started to argue, then reminded himself that she had a stake in this, too. And he needed to stay nearby in case she had another vision or ran into her brother.

She shut the door firmly and hurried up the fire station's drive, her shadow lengthening in the flood-lights shining from above the door. In seconds she had disappeared from sight.

Sharp-edged desire clawed through him. He wanted her, but being with her would never be just sex for him. For every man there was a woman he couldn't walk away from, and for him that woman was Cass Hollister. She'd done the walking last time, and he'd been feeling the pain of it all over again since seeing her in that hospital bed.

He groaned, dropping his head back against the seat. Why had he let her kiss him? Why had he kissed her back? Now he'd had a taste of her, and it was going to torment him.

He'd been kidding himself to think he could treat her like any other victim. She wasn't just any victim. She was the woman who'd ripped out his heart. That was what he needed to remember.

Chapter 4

The man could still make her melt. Cass had ordered herself not to think about that kiss. She lasted ten whole seconds before the memory was all over her. He wanted her, but he'd said they weren't going back there, and she knew he meant it.

Now, sitting with him again in the SUV, her body still tingling from his kiss, he was aloof. She reminded herself that however cold he was now, he'd been there for her earlier when she'd needed him.

He'd changed from his slacks and dress shirt to jeans and a black T-shirt that molded to his broad shoulders and flat stomach. Soft, worn denim hugged his powerful thighs. He smelled good, like mint and shaving cream. His left hand was draped over the steering wheel; his right rested on his thigh.

As much as his kiss had wound Cass up, something else was zinging along her nerves now. After placing her camera on the console, she slid a pink slip of paper out of her shorts pocket. "There was a message from Lee when I got to the firehouse."

"What?" Ben's head whipped toward her. "What kind of message?"

"Just to say he was checking on me." There was no telling what that meant, and she shuddered. Her brother could be watching her. Or maybe he just wanted her to think he was.

"You're sure it was from him?"

"Yes. He left his name. Isn't that helpful?" she choked out. "I called his parole officer, Hugo. He still hasn't heard from Lee or seen him."

Ben cursed. "You okay?"

"Yes." Just looking at his mouth roused a tickle in her stomach. "At least he didn't come to the firehouse, although that might've been better. If he had, we'd know for sure he was in town."

"My gut says he is, and yeah, I know that doesn't prove anything."

He took the ramp from Britton Road onto northbound Hefner Parkway. "We'll find him, Cass. He's probably still in Oklahoma City and watching you, just like he wants you to think." Ben exited on Memorial Road then took the Kilpatrick Turnpike west. "I haven't had a chance to print the picture of your blisters yet."

"That's okay." The memory of her ravaged palms made her slightly nauseous. And no matter what Ben said, she felt like a freak.

He hitched a thumb toward the backseat. "I brought the files on the two fires you…saw before they started."

Cass unbuckled her seat belt and turned in her seat, leaning over to grab the folders. As she eased back down, she felt Ben's gaze on her backside. Sensation fluttered in her belly again.

He hit the overhead light as she opened the files and read. "The first one was started with a matchbook. The second with gasoline. The torch didn't even try to hide the gas can.

"We didn't get any prints at either site, so we still don't have a solid lead. I interviewed people in the area, but no one saw anything."

She exhaled in exasperation. "Since the blazes weren't started the same way, how will we know if one person is responsible for them?"

"We won't for sure until we catch him, but I think it's one torch. Just call it my gut again."

A sudden frustration surged through her. Why couldn't this…curse, gift, whatever it was, go away as suddenly as it had come? On second thought, if she had to die again in order to get rid of it, forget it.

Ben drove up to a complex of four quadrants, each one hosting a single strip of three offices, some of them already open for business, judging by the signs. "There's not much around here we can use for cover."

She scanned the well-lit parking lot and the empty field beyond, which was dotted with pine trees and scrub brush. Bradford pear trees lined the median dividing the complex into its four sections.

At the second quadrant, Ben drove over a curb,

positioning his SUV behind a completed office that sat diagonal to the nearly finished building Cass recognized as the scene of the next fire.

"We won't be immediately visible here," he said as he killed the engine. "Can't run the air conditioner, so you should roll down your window."

Cass did, wondering if her coming had been a good idea. Who knew how long she would have to sit here with Ben and remember their mind-blowing kiss. And realize for the hundredth time just how badly her judgment sucked. Her ex-boyfriend had been a dirty cop, and she'd never suspected a thing. She'd stayed too long with a guy who was a jerk and run from the one who wasn't.

Ben grabbed his camcorder case from the backseat and pulled out the charger for the extra battery, then plugged it into the cigarette lighter.

"The other fires I saw were at night," she said. "Hopefully this one will be, too."

Nodding, he aimed the camera, then repositioned himself to get another angle. Once he was satisfied, he leaned back against the seat.

After they ate the sandwiches Cass had brought, they sat quietly. The night sounds of crickets and locusts swelled around them. From the nearby expressway, she could hear the whoosh of passing automobiles.

Maybe she was paranoid, but Ben seemed determined not to touch her in any way. He had pulled back from the glancing brush of her fingers when she'd handed him a sandwich, and again when she offered him a bottled water.

In spite of that—or maybe because of it—she was acutely aware of him. His long fingers resting on the steering wheel, the small space separating his big frame from hers, his body heat. The urge to kiss him again surged inside her. And when she caught his gaze on her mouth, awareness drummed against her already ragged nerves.

In the shadows, his blue eyes looked black, sultry. Even with the window open and the smells of grass, fuel and dirt in the air, she caught his masculine woodsy scent. Sitting a foot away, wrapped in darkness, the drift of his body heat was almost palpable against her skin.

Her heart hurt thinking about how right their kiss had felt. And how he had pulled back. "I'm sorry if I was out of line earlier."

The way his eyes narrowed told her he knew exactly what she was referring to.

"It's okay." His words notwithstanding, his tone clearly said "drop it."

"It only occurred to me later that you might be seeing someone."

He shifted his gaze out the windshield, his body rigid, his profile softened by the night. Silence swelled between them. Had she ruined everything? Even the smooth way they had been working together?

"I wasn't trying to make a move on you. Or, well—" She gave a nervous laugh. "That wasn't my intent. Things got out of hand. I just needed—" *You.* She bit back the word. "A friend."

He looked at her, eyes glittering hotly. The mix

of light and shadow shifting across his face made him appear harsh, intimidating.

She tried not to squirm. "I guess I just wasn't thinking."

"Forget it," he said gruffly. "I know you were upset by the episode at the cemetery."

"I didn't mean to do it, but I'm not sorry."

Wariness flared in his gaze. "What am I supposed to say here?"

"Nothing." A nervous breath shuddered out of her. "I'm just...clearing the air."

She might as well face up to everything. "And while I'm on the subject of things neither of us wants to talk about, I don't think I've ever apologized for walking away from you. Running away is more accurate, I guess."

His gaze moved over her face, lingered on her mouth. Hope ballooned inside her until he broke the moment by picking up the camcorder and staring through the viewfinder.

Before now, she hadn't allowed herself to consider the possibility that they might still be together if she hadn't panicked at the first sign of commitment. "You ever wonder what might've happened with us?"

"No." Despite a brief hesitation, he sounded certain.

Was he relieved now that she hadn't moved in with him? "At the time, I didn't realize how much I was hurting you. All I thought about was—"

"Getting away," he grumbled. "Yeah, I picked up on that."

"I was messed up, Ben. Did you understand why I left?"

"You didn't trust me not to hurt you."

"No! It was because I didn't trust myself. I was worried about making another mistake that would hurt both of us." She hated that he ever believed he'd been at fault. "After Mitch was busted, I was afraid to rely on my judgment about anything." Her boyfriend of nearly two years had been a dirty cop on the take and she had suspected nothing until his arrest.

"Then you and I met three weeks later, and I fell hard for you. And fast. I left because it scared me."

His eyes narrowed.

Since he was listening, Cass tentatively continued, "Have you been able to forgive me?"

Tension strummed across her nerves. The sweat slicking her palms had nothing to do with the hot July night and everything to do with the big man sitting less than an arm's length away.

"Yeah. And I think you were probably right. We moved too fast."

Did that mean he hadn't felt as strongly about her as he'd thought? She had no right to feel disappointed.

"I figured I'd done something," he admitted hesitantly. "For a long time, I wondered what, then I realized it wasn't really about me. Not for the most part, anyway."

"None of it was. There was nothing bad about you." She folded one leg under her. "You were great."

He stared at her mouth, then, with an impatient shake of his head, dragged a hand down his face. "I pushed. You weren't ready."

"I *wasn't* ready, but you didn't push. I accused you of that because I was afraid. I didn't believe my feelings for you could be real, not so fast. I wasn't sure if what we had was only physical. If I made you feel my problems were about you, I apologize for that, too." She took a deep breath. "Being with you was the only right thing I did during those months after Mitch."

"Not right enough, I guess."

She managed not to reach for his hand. Tension was already palpable. Touching him wasn't a good idea. "You've been there for me since all this weirdness started, and I appreciate it. You're a great guy." *And I was an idiot to throw that away.*

"I like you all right, too," he said gruffly, looking uncomfortable at the compliment.

Her pulse skittered. For an instant she saw a raw hunger in his eyes. Then it disappeared as he shifted his gaze back out the windshield. The desire she'd glimpsed prompted her to ask, "So... did I step on another woman's toes when I kissed you?"

"No."

Did that mean he was seeing someone, but not seriously? Or that he wasn't seeing anyone at all?

Frustrated, she searched his face. She could tell nothing from his neutral tone, but she certainly saw no hint of the skin-tingling desire she'd seen earlier. He'd moved on; she had to do the same.

"Can we start over from here? As friends?"

He shifted until his gaze held hers once again. Indecision and doubt flickered across his face. Regret swept through her.

The leashed energy in his body told her that he

was restraining himself, but the shrug he gave was nonchalant. "Sure, friends."

She'd thought addressing the kiss and the issues between them would erase the dissatisfaction that had gnawed at her since seeing him again, but it hadn't.

Suddenly he leaned forward, grabbing the video camera.

Snatching up her own camera, Cass whispered, "Did you see someone?"

He turned the camera on and looked through the viewfinder. "Some*thing*. Not a person." Then, "Smoke!"

Cass saw a sudden orange glow in the building they were watching. A heartbeat later, flames crawled out two side windows.

"Damn it!" Ben sprang out of the SUV, still holding the video camera. "Check the other buildings!"

He took off running as Cass scrambled out behind him. Sprinting toward the nearest building, she fumbled her cell phone from her pocket and dialed 9-1-1. She pounded on the door of a dentist's office, yelling for anyone there to get out, then moved on. Due to the late hour, no employees were likely to be around, but vagrants were a different story.

Moments later she heard sirens, then the blaring horns of fire trucks. There was no sign of anyone, which meant the torch had either come and gone before they'd arrived or had eluded their notice.

The firefighters were soon directing water on the blaze. By the time Cass finished checking the last building, the fire was out.

An hour later, after giving their information to the incident commander, Ben dropped her off at the firehouse. He wanted to start his investigation immediately and promised he would let her know what he found.

As she walked inside, she hoped he would find something to indicate whether Lee was responsible for tonight's fire or any of the others.

But upstairs, in the women's bunk room, she was the one who found something. A walnut plaque with gold engraving lay in the center of her bed, with a small piece of paper taped to it. A sudden inexplicable dread pounded at her as she drew closer. She recognized that plaque. It was an award from the city to her father for distinguished service. One of several awards he'd been given, all of which she kept at her house.

Legs going numb, her gaze slid to the attached paper.

What did you think about the fire show tonight?

It was her brother's handwriting. How had he walked into the firehouse unnoticed? How had he known she wasn't here?

He had to have been watching her. Did he know she had seen his fire before it started? No, he couldn't.

Shaken, she stared at the plaque. Her brother was messing with her mind. Again.

It was 3:30 a.m. when Ben picked her up at the station. "You all right?"

"Yes." He'd asked her that same question twice

when she'd called him about finding her father's award on her bed. Of course she'd been rattled then, but she was calm now. Mostly.

Ben insisted it would be a good idea to check her house for evidence of a break-in, even though Cass felt sure there would be none. Her brother would know how to get inside their childhood home without force.

Sure enough, they found no signs of unlawful entry at the three-bedroom house where she and Lee had grown up. She unlocked the door and followed Ben inside.

"After I found the plaque, I called Lee's parole officer again. I probably should've waited until he got to the office, but I couldn't, so I tracked down his home number. Hugo said he still hasn't seen or heard from my brother."

"Not surprising," Ben muttered.

"He also said he was keeping notes of everything."

"That's good. His account will support ours."

"I woke the guys, and they all said they hadn't seen anyone come in or go out of the firehouse. Did you find anything at the scene?"

"It was definitely arson. Found the base of a lamp and shattered lightbulb glass. I'll have to check some samples to be sure, but I think the lightbulb was injected with gasoline, then the lamp put on a timer. That allowed the torch to get far away, giving him an alibi. When the bulb got hot enough to explode, it ignited a nearby trail of gasoline."

"So everything could've been arranged hours before we got there."

"And probably was."

Frustrated, she huffed out a breath. "Why couldn't I have seen *that* in one of my visions?"

None of Cass's family pictures or furniture was disturbed. Only the one plaque was missing from her father's collection.

There was nothing suspicious until they stepped into the dining area, where a framed photograph of her and her father lay on the table. Next to it was a key.

Chilled, she turned to Ben. "He's been here."

"How do you know?" He came up beside her, his arm touching hers.

"The photograph is out of place. It's my favorite and Lee knows it." For one second she let herself lean into him. She gestured toward the table. "Plus, that's my extra house key. The only other person with a key is Jana, and she wouldn't come here unless I asked her to, and she wouldn't leave her key. Lee would be able to figure out where to find the spare key. I know that isn't enough for you, but it's enough for me." She wrapped her arms around herself. "It's Lee."

"I sure can't prove it isn't," he said stonily.

Nothing else in or around the house was disturbed. Ben sealed and marked the photograph and key in separate evidence bags, saying he would have them checked for prints.

She didn't want to go back to the firehouse, but she certainly couldn't stay here. Maybe a hotel.

Taking a last look around Cass's small house, he wrapped one hand around her upper arm. "You're coming home with me."

In some ways, she would feel safer with him. In other ways, she wouldn't. Especially after their kiss. "Do you think that's a good idea?"

"Doesn't matter if it is or not. Your brother isn't getting anywhere near you."

The tight line of his lips, the burning resolve in his eyes, told her not to argue. So she didn't.

Chapter 5

Cass couldn't sleep. She was hot. She was mad. She wanted to pound Lee. And she just plain *wanted* Ben.

Part of her thrilled to his protectiveness, but another part of her chafed. His hauling her home with him made her want more than friendship. Especially since memories were everywhere.

She remembered making love in front of the fireplace. In the kitchen. Their first time had been in the hallway outside his bedroom. They had dated for about two weeks when he brought her to his house after his family's annual Labor Day cookout. As he was showing her around, he kissed her and it just happened.

She could still feel the uneven texture of the wall

at her back, the plush carpet between her toes. His mouth *all over her*. The recollection caused a flutter low in her belly. Exactly what she didn't need.

Cass got out of bed. Eyes adjusting to the darkness, she padded barefoot down the carpeted hallway to Ben's living room. The guest bedroom was on the other side of the house from his, so at least she wasn't worried about waking him. Moonlight drifted over the fireplace and mantel, and the dark blue recliner at one end of the navy tweed sofa.

She crossed the taupe carpet and stopped at the French doors leading to the back porch. Built-in bookcases lined the wall to her left, adjacent to a fireplace. Sweat dampened her neck, trickled between her breasts. She lifted her hair and twisted it on top of her head, fanning herself with her free hand.

Her brother was out there somewhere, watching her. Waiting for something. What? Thinking about the award he'd taken from their childhood home, the key and photograph he'd left, had tension knotting her shoulders. She didn't want to believe Lee was the one setting fires and tormenting her, the one who had tried to kill her, the one who had killed a child, but she knew it was him. He had motive, means and opportunity. Who else could it be?

She'd been so glad it was Ben who'd been with her at her house. Beneath the desire, she felt safe with him and always had. Another realization she'd come to in the months since walking away from him.

The throb that started in her veins every time she thought about him had her moving to the fireplace. She released her hair and dragged it over her shoulder. A framed photograph of Ben with his brother, Jeff, sat on the mantel. The candid shot of the pair laughing clearly showed the closeness between them.

She and Lee had once been close. Until he'd failed the fire academy and their relationship had become a twisted competition.

"Cass?"

Jumping, she whirled at the sound of Ben's deep, sleep-roughened voice.

"Didn't mean to startle you."

"That's okay. I'm sorry if I woke you."

"You didn't. Wasn't really getting much sleep." Dragging a hand down his face, he moved into the room and stopped behind the couch.

Pale light washed over him, bringing his bare chest into sharp definition. The dark shorts he wore emphasized the bands of muscle across his stomach. His gaze roamed over her, making her keenly aware that she wore only panties and one of his T-shirts. She felt a rush in her blood.

"You see another fire? Are your hands blistered?"

"No, I'm fine." He sounded so matter-of-fact. As if he were asking about a headache.

Her emotions rocketed between anger and lust. If she stayed out here with him, she wasn't sure she could hold herself together.

He stepped around the sofa and walked toward her. Light and shadow skimmed over his wide shoulders, the flex of muscle in his arms and legs. The sight of his deep chest, the black hair that thinned between his breastbone and toward his navel, had her swallowing hard. An ache started at her center. She should go back to bed. Right now. Alone.

He stopped a foot away, his eyes gleaming in the dim light. "Is Lee the reason you can't sleep?"

"Partly." She wasn't about to tell him that he was the other reason. "I don't understand why he's doing this. I know he wants revenge for whatever he thinks Dad did to him and for my helping to send him to prison." Her voice cracked. "But he could take out plenty of resentment without setting fires and…and killing a kid."

"He won't get close to you again." Ben shifted, coming nearer and sparking all her nerve endings. He smelled like a summer night. He was all muscle and hard man and power.

She dug her nails into her palms to keep from touching him.

"Until we catch him, you won't be alone," he went on. "I'll be with you, or a cop will be assigned to protect you. The fire chief okayed it, and so did the chief of police." He toyed with a strand of hair lying over her shoulder.

Trying not to look at his mouth, she focused on the hollow of his strong throat. "Staying with me 24/7 will drive you crazy."

"Probably," he murmured. He didn't look as if he minded.

Easing close enough that she felt his body heat, he braced his left hand on the mantel just above her shoulder. "Every time I think about Lee in the firehouse, how easily he could've gotten to you, it makes me furious."

"Same here." Her pulse thundered wildly at Ben's nearness. "And he scares me."

"I won't let anything happen to you, Cass."

She wanted to throw herself at him, wrap herself around him. Naked. All she said was, "Thanks."

"Mmm." His gaze drifted over her, triggering points of sensation under her skin.

Go. Now. Her mind screamed the words, but she couldn't move.

"I made a mistake."

She stilled. "By bringing me home with you?"

"No, not about that." The low gruffness of his voice made her shiver. Fierce emotion blazed in his eyes. He looked almost savage. Dangerous. Her pulse skittered.

"About saying I wanted to move on as friends. That's not going to work for me."

Her heart sank. He really hadn't forgiven her for what she'd done. "I understand. I'll go tomorrow."

She had no idea where. Sadness tightened her throat.

"I want more than that."

At his husky words, she blinked. "What?"

He angled his body so she was backed into the mantel. His other hand clamped over the dark wood, caging her in.

Hardly daring to breath, she glanced to either side. His hands were big. His forearms were corded with muscle, dusted with dark hair. He leaned in, his body not touching hers, yet raising prickles of awareness clear down to her toes. Need tugged low in her belly.

He couldn't mean what she thought he did. Their kiss hours ago had scrambled her brain. She was misreading the signals. "You want more what?"

"You." He bent his head and brushed his mouth against hers. "I want more of you."

"Oh." A little wobbly, she hooked a hand into his waistband to steady herself.

The light scrape of her nails against his abdomen had all the muscles in Ben's body clenching. The moonlight covered her like a veil, giving her skin a translucent glow.

Her eyes darkened. "Really? But you said—"

"I was wrong."

After a long moment that had his nerves winding tight, she asked softly, "Are you sure?"

"Oh, yeah." The fact that she had hurt him was fading into nonexistence next to the raging intensity of desire. After learning her brother had somehow gotten into the firehouse, Ben's protective instinct had kicked into hyper-mode. That tipped the scales for him.

He'd tried to forget that kiss, tried to forget *her*, but their time together in his vehicle had weakened his restraint. When he'd seen her standing there in his T-shirt, the curve of her body outlined in the moonlight, her full breasts pressing against the thin cotton, he'd said to hell with it. He had to get his hands on her.

In the seconds since he'd told her what he wanted, she hadn't tried to leave. And she hadn't pushed him away. That and her slightly parted lips were enough invitation for him. He kissed her again, harder.

Her arms went around his neck, and he slanted his mouth over hers, going deeper into that velvet heat. While they had been checking her house for signs of a break-in, an urgency had built inside him. Now, with her finally in his arms, it leveled out.

Breathing in the subtle scents of her soap and his, he homed in on the layer of cotton between them, the pressure of her nipples against his chest.

One hand curved around her nape. He skimmed the other over her bottom to the back of her thigh, dying to feel more of her. He picked her up, and she wrapped her legs around his waist.

Cradled by her thighs, all his blood rushed south. Her hands were in his hair, her mouth was hot on his. If possible, his sex grew even more rigid and his legs grew weaker.

Still carrying her, he moved to the couch and sank down, his knee bumping the coffee table. Without breaking the kiss, he buried his hands in her hair and ravaged her mouth. Thick silky locks tickled his thighs when he nudged her head back to rake his teeth down her throat.

She wiggled, fitting herself to him. The low sound of pleasure that escaped her flicked his nerves like a whip.

Half-dazed by the honey-sweet taste of her mouth, the delicate scent of woman and soap, he reached under the thin T-shirt, skating his hands over her bottom, the gentle flare of her hips.

She pressed down hard on his erection as she dragged her mouth along his cheek to nip his earlobe. When she sucked at a spot low on his neck, he hissed out a breath. Despite the coolness of the room, sweat dampened Ben's chest. The only sounds in the house were their labored breaths and the occasional moan.

He slid his fingers around to her rib cage and palmed her full breasts. She shuddered in his lap, making him even harder. Thumbing her tight nipples, he pulled back from the kiss, shoving up the shirt so he could see her plump creamy flesh.

Her breathing was as labored as his. Her eyes fluttered open, and the total surrender there nearly had him ripping off her underwear. Lashes lowering, she watched him touch her, and that charged him up even more. Even in the silvery light, he could see the flush of arousal on her skin. Could feel it, too.

She fit him the way she always had, the way he knew she would. He pressed a hot, openmouthed kiss on the swell of her breast, then slid his tongue to where pale flesh met rosy-pink.

As he closed his mouth over her, she touched his face. "Ben," she rasped.

Heat shot through him. He knew what she liked. How fast, how slow. Every damn thing about her, but he didn't know how long he could hold out. When she slid her hands to his waistband and pushed down his shorts and boxers together, he nearly lost it. He eased up, and she scooted back on his thighs to tug the garments far enough out of the way to free him. She wrapped her hand around him, making a soft sound that chewed at his tenuous control.

He swept one hand up her sleek outer thigh, then inside to dip his fingers into the burning hot crease where her hip met her groin. She moaned or he did. He couldn't tell, didn't care. Man, she made him hurt to be inside her. Now.

She went up on her knees, reaching to push off her panties.

"No," he murmured against her breast, hooking a

finger into a leg opening and pulling the lacy fabric to the side.

The silky liquid heat against his knuckle told him she was ready. With his free hand, he grasped her hip and pulled her onto him. She sank down with a gasp, her arms tightening around his neck. For a second, his vision blurred. She rested her forehead against his, his name spilling from her throat in a ragged plea.

When she moved, Ben caught her rhythm, fast, intense, almost desperate. He wanted to protect her, claim her. Take her. The stroke of his body inside hers, the tease of her breasts, the friction of her panties rubbing against both of them, splintered his control.

Gritting his teeth, he managed to hold off his own release until he felt her inner muscles clench around him, and then he let go.

Over the next three days, Cass and Ben settled into a rhythm. They jogged in the mornings and ate together every night. When Ben went out to check leads or deal with other cases on his desk, an OCPD officer stayed with Cass.

She hadn't had a vision since the night they'd first made love. Ben had remarked on it that morning, and she had told him not to jinx it by talking about it.

An hour ago, he'd come home from a night of working a fire scene, talked to the cop assigned to her, then eaten. It was nearly noon by the time he took a shower. Cass debated going in with him, then plopped down on his big oak bed to wait, one finger tracing the pattern in his blue plaid comforter. The familiar gray walls and white trim were reassuring, a constant in her upside-down world.

Being here made her feel shielded from her brother and the visions. She felt as if she belonged here, although she wasn't about to tell Ben that. She was afraid he might say what was happening between them didn't mean to him what it meant to her.

He walked out of the bathroom, his hair still damp, his boxers riding low. Her gaze slid down his dark-haired chest to the flat of his stomach. He grinned and flopped down beside her. Shifting to his side, he propped himself up on one elbow and hooked an arm around her waist to pull her to him. "Hey, gorgeous."

"Hey."

After a long kiss, he rolled to his back and arranged her body half on top of his. "The picture from the cell phone is still where I left it on the kitchen counter. Have you looked at it since I brought it home?"

"No. I'll look at it when I follow up with Dr. Hill tomorrow." She nuzzled his neck, inhaling the delicious scent of man and soap. "Let's not talk about that."

"What do you want to talk about, then?" His voice was gravelly with fatigue. He slipped a hand under the hem of her red spaghetti-strapped T-shirt, tickling the small of her back.

"Nothing." She raked her nails up the inside of his thigh and felt a muscle jerk beneath her touch. "I don't want to talk at all. Unless you're too tired to get naked."

A laugh rumbled out of him, and before she could blink, he had her on her back and was pressing himself against her. "Does that feel tired to you?"

"Yes. Maybe you should rest." She laughed. "Let's take a nap."

"Not until you finish what you started, woman." The husky growl of his voice shot heat straight to her toes.

He brushed his lips across her forehead, her eyelids, her cheeks, before slowly seducing her mouth.

She ran her hands over his hard wide shoulders as he dragged his mouth to her ear, his hot breath causing a shiver deep down inside. Just as she had last night, Cass wished he would ask if she wanted more than this, but she knew he wouldn't.

Which was fine, she told herself, as he peeled down her ribbed knit top and curled his tongue around one nipple. A shiver rippled through her. She slid her hands into his hair, giving herself over to the feel of his hot mouth on her, his heavy weight pressing her into the mattress.

Easing to one side, he undid the button of her denim shorts, and brushed his thumb back and forth just inside the waistband of her panties.

Her breathing broke. "Ben."

He looked up, blue eyes glittering. Dark color streaked his cheekbones. With his blunt fingertips, he nudged her hair back and stroked her face.

The scent of soap and musk settled in her lungs. His touch was like a drug, drawing her into a place where there was only sensation. The solid angles of his body next to her softness. The crisp hair of his chest tickling her skin. His gentle finger down her neck. The brush of a knuckle along the full undersides of her breasts.

There was no mistaking the possessiveness blazing in his eyes, or the tenderness and desire.

Throat tight with emotion, she framed his face in her hands, skimming her thumbs along his lightly whiskered jaw. Covering her mouth with his, he eased his palm into her panties and cupped her. She arched against him, murmuring encouragement.

Abruptly, a flare of orange burned across her mind.

Cass's pulse spiked, and her legs tightened reflexively around his hand. No! Not now!

Fighting the vision, she focused on Ben's hot tongue tasting her body, on the intimate way he massaged her. Another fiery image flashed in her brain.

She refused to let it take her this time. Trying not to panic, she locked her gaze with his. Hoping their connection would be strong enough to stave off the vision, she kissed him roughly, almost desperately.

Not now. Not now. Not now.

Powerless, she felt herself sliding away.

And then she was standing in the middle of a fire. Flames shot toward the ceiling. Gray and white smoke swirled around her. Crayon drawings were taped to walls painted with a safari motif. Small desks, illegible words on a chalkboard. A clock above the door.

The flames lashed at her hands as she dropped to her stomach, searching for an escape.

Alarms clanged through the building. Oxygen tank weighting her back, Cass crawled into the hallway, relieved to see no children. She searched frantically for a red exit sign, her hands beginning to roast. Where were her gloves? As she looked down, her skin peeled back.

"Cass! Cass!" Ben was shaking her, yelling her name.

Disoriented, terrified, she stared dumbly at him. Her palms throbbed in white-hot agony. Ben still lay on top of her. And her hands still held his face. Her bloody blistered hands.

Crying out in horror, she jerked them away.

Agony shot up her arms. Panic nearly choked her.

Cass's breath jammed in her chest. Ben sat up, scooping her into his lap. One strong arm curved around her waist. His other hand pressed her head to his chest.

Uncaring how much it hurt, she drew her hands against her body so they wouldn't touch him. Finally the pain began to fade.

And there was Ben, solid, steady, holding her tight against him. "Are you okay?"

She nodded jerkily.

"Let me see your hands."

"N-no." Tears burned down her cheeks. It made her stomach churn that this had happened now. *In bed with him.*

She trembled, dragging in air as Ben sat her beside him. He smoothed her hair away from her sweat-dampened face. "I'm going to get a wet rag, then I want to look at your hands."

As he moved into the bathroom, she stared down at her palms, relieved to see that they were fine, then, in the next second, she was furious.

During sex! If the visions could hit her at a time like this, they could happen anytime. Anywhere.

Pressure squeezed her chest. She was a sideshow freak, and she might have to deal with these hideous episodes the rest of her life.

She managed to get to her feet and tug on her shorts. Legs shaking, she readjusted her T-shirt. He was taking a long time. Why wouldn't he? He was probably repulsed. And as disturbed as she was.

When he returned with a wet cloth, she couldn't look at him. Very gently, he examined her hands, kissing her palms before running the rag softly over her face.

Tears stung her eyes.

"Tell me what happened."

She tried to control the tremor in her voice. "One minute we were kissing, then I was in the middle of a fire. At a nursery school. Flames everywhere, but there were no children. And the next thing I knew my... hands were on your face. My...disgusting hands. And you were staring down at me, white as a sheet."

"You scared the hell out of me."

And probably sickened him, too. She choked back a sob and stepped around him.

"I hate that I couldn't help you." He watched her pace the width of his room.

She waited for him to say more, to distance himself from her. When there was only silence, she dared a look at him.

Concern shadowed his eyes. But even if he weren't revolted now, what about next time?

"I can't do this. I thought I could, but I can't."

"Can't do what?"

"Be with you."

He went still. "Cass."

She resumed her pacing. "How can you stand to look at me? I'm a freak!"

"Stop saying that." Snagging her elbow, he held her in place, waiting until her gaze met his. Her eyes were wild, fever-bright. His chest ached. Ben stroked her cheek, and she jerked away as if it hurt to be touched. "You're not a freak."

"The fact that I might go into some kind of… trance while we're having sex says I am." She put a hand over her mouth. "This is horrifying in so many ways, I don't even know where to begin. I can't put you through that."

"Stop." He took her shoulders. "There's no reason to walk away."

"No reason? I'm terrified at the thought of being naked with you and that happening again. I tried to stop it, and I couldn't control it at all. What if I have these episodes the rest of my life?"

"We'll deal with it."

"Haven't I put you through enough?" Her voice was bitter as she turned away.

He wrapped his arms around her from behind. "Cass."

She stiffened.

"Listen to me." Ignoring the rigid line of her spine, he nuzzled her petal-smooth cheek. "It scared you. It scared me, too, but it's over."

"For now." She dashed a hand under her eyes.

"But you…you can't get involved with someone who could go zinging off into a trance any second."

"We're already involved." He tried to remain calm. "And we can handle this if we do it together."

"Ben." Her voice cracked. "I can't."

Anger flared. He dropped his arms and stepped away. "You mean you *won't.*"

She was upset. He didn't blame her, but getting rid of him wasn't the way to deal with it. That seemed to be her answer to everything.

Which pissed him off. Hands curling into fists, he fought to keep his voice level. "You're using what just happened as an excuse."

She turned, looking confused. "An excuse for what?"

"To take off. I thought we were past that. You think I'm getting too close, so you're ready to run."

"This isn't about that at all."

He ignored the pain in her eyes. "If it weren't, you'd want us to work this out together."

"You have no idea what you'd be signing up for."

"Neither do you. Something could happen to me, too. I could get hurt or sick, so what's the difference? You're running because you feel you're getting in too deep with me, and it scares you."

"What if…the visions start coming all the time? And not just when we're alone but out in public? I'd become a burden."

"You wouldn't be more of a pain in the butt than you are right now," he muttered.

"No?" Her eyes flashed. "What if sometime we're together with your family and I zone out? What will you tell them? 'Oh, by the way, she has—'" she hooked her fingers in the air "'—*visions*. Just give us a minute.'"

"Stop it." He wanted to shake her, so he braced his hands on his hips. "Cut the bull, Cass, and call this what it really is."

"What do you mean?"

"You can't commit. Or you won't. Things have been going great, and now you're running out on me. Just like last time."

Hurt darkened her eyes. "That was different."

His jaw tightened. He knew his next words were harsh, but he had to get through to her. "We get to a certain point and then you can't seem to get any further. You don't try to work through things. You leave."

"I'm doing this for you."

"Enough!" He yanked his jeans off the floor and jerked them on. He had to get out of here, had to cool down. "We're not doing this right now."

"*What?*" Disbelief, then anger, streaked across her features.

He tried to gentle his voice, but even *he* flinched at the roughness of his tone. "We need to step back for a minute, then talk about this later, when it isn't so fresh."

Chin tilted mutinously, she plainly wanted to argue, but after a long minute, she gave a sharp nod.

Ben wasn't dumb enough to feel relief. She had something wedged in her brain and wouldn't let go, but for now, they had to take a breather. "You saw the next fire. That means we need to get there. Tell me where."

As he pulled on a navy T-shirt, she said, "Buttonwood Pre-school. The name was written above the blackboard. And I saw a clock."

"A clock? You haven't seen anything like that before."

"It read five-fifty-six. Do you think that matters?"

"So far, all the stuff you've seen at the other fires has been accurate. That could be a.m. or p.m., though."

He fastened his jeans and grabbed his tennis shoes as she put on her own shoes. They would deal with this fire. Then Ben would deal with her. "We'd better get moving."

Color high, mouth tight, she silently followed him out the door.

After gathering what they needed, they drove to the preschool on the far west side of Oklahoma City. The air hummed with tension.

It wasn't until they reached the school and had their cameras set up that she spoke. "Why are you fighting me on this? Breaking up is the best thing for both of us."

"It's the *easiest*," he emphasized harshly, trying to be patient. "Not the *best*."

"I think I'm doing the right thing."

"You thought that last time, too. Easy, hard, it doesn't matter. I'll tell you this. I'm not letting you go, and you need to find a way to deal with *that*."

Chapter 6

The school building was constructed as an open-ended rectangle with a grassy berm in the center leading to the playground. The corner of the roof where Ben and Cass sat hidden afforded a view of all the classrooms on both sides of the structure.

They hadn't spoken for the last two hours. Ben was still fuming because Cass was again trying to bolt. From the rigid set of her shoulders, she was still upset, too. Probably about his telling her how things were going to be.

He knew the visions were traumatic. And, hell yes, the mid-coital episode had freaked him out, too. But neither of those things was a reason to dump him. *Again.* He knew she had feelings for him. What he didn't know was how to make her trust them.

Frustrated, he admitted to himself that he might have pushed too hard.

Catching a movement out of the corner of his eye, Ben scanned the grassy area between the long sides of the building. There it was again, a motion in the shadows beneath the eaves in the glare of the late afternoon sun. He turned on the video camera.

A couple of feet from him, Cass sat with camera ready. As they watched, the form moved. Something whizzed through the air and crashed through a window on the opposite side of the building. Cass snapped pictures as Ben followed another blur with the video camera. Glinting in the light, the object hurtled through the broken window, landed inside and exploded.

Molotov cocktail, Ben registered, as Cass called 9-1-1. The camera's zoom on its most powerful setting, he followed the suspect as he ran away from the building and onto the playground. When the culprit stopped to look back at the flames now curling out the broken window, Ben could tell it was a man. "We got him."

The man took off again, weaving through a swing set.

Beside Ben, Cass continued to take pictures. "I can't tell if it's Lee."

Ben kept recording until the suspect disappeared into a stand of trees.

Thanks to the approval he had gotten to put the nearest firehouse on standby, trucks rumbled into the parking lot within mere minutes.

He and Cass gathered their empty sandwich bags

and water bottles, then climbed down the ladder they'd leaned against the side of the building.

As the firefighters rolled out hoses and rushed toward the flames, Ben updated the incident commander and replayed the video for him and Cass. Though they all agreed the suspect was male, none of them could distinguish specific features.

He and Cass gave their statements and left the scene. As they drove, Ben arranged for the cop guarding her to meet them at her firehouse. Once she picked up some necessary paperwork for her doctor's visit, Officer Giles would take her for a checkup at the emergency room.

As she slid out of the SUV, Ben knew that things between them were still strained. He didn't like it, but he figured he'd said enough for now.

He cleared his throat. "Hopefully, the police lab will be able to get a clear image once they blow up the video."

She nodded.

"Giles will take you back to my house after you see Dr. Hill. I'll call you as soon as I learn anything."

"Great." She closed the door and turned toward the firehouse.

As he drove away, he glanced in his rearview mirror until she disappeared from sight. His chest hurt. He'd finally convinced himself to let her back in, and now he might have sabotaged the relationship. Maybe he'd been too caveman back in his bedroom. Had he screwed up everything? What if he had run her off for good?

About two minutes later, his cell phone rang.

Glancing at the screen, he saw it was Cass and answered, hoping she would tell him she'd decided he was right. Or that she was at least willing to try. "Hey."

"Ben?"

The slight tremor in her voice had his spine turning into steel. "What is it? What's wrong?"

"My brother—"

"Come to Cass's house," an unfamiliar masculine voice said. "And bring the video."

Damn it, how had Lee Hollister gotten to Cass?

"We'll make a swap."

"Let me talk to her," Ben snarled.

"Come alone."

"Don't hurt her, you sonova—"

Click. Dial tone.

Ben cursed as rage hazed his vision. It took him a moment to react, then he made a sharp U-turn and drove like hell to Cass's home. On the way, he called for police backup, then fire dispatch, warning both of them to keep their distance, and to run without sirens and lights, so Lee wouldn't spot them. How had Hollister gotten close to her at the firehouse? Where was Officer Giles?

Fear cut straight through Ben. There had been no time to book the video into evidence, no time to make a copy. He just hoped there was time to reach Cass before her pyromaniac brother finished what he'd started at that downtown hotel.

"He'll be right over." Cass's brother dropped her cell phone beside her on the leather sofa.

He had forced her into her Mustang by drilling a gun into the side of her head. A gun that likely belonged to Officer Giles—and she could only hope that Lee hadn't killed him to get it.

Cass refused to cry and focused instead on fury. Some part of her had wanted to believe he hadn't been the one who tried to kill her, but the weapon he stuck in her face crushed that hope.

"Why use the house where we grew up, Lee?" She had to do something, but what? Her hands and feet were bound with duct tape. "Why not someplace where people won't recognize you if you're seen?"

"Everything started here." Her brother's eyes, the same green as hers, glittered like shards of glass. They also shared the same ginger hair color, but that was where the similarities stopped. He had always been the more introverted, and as they grew older, he became more so, to the point that, before going to prison, he'd withdrawn from most people. "This is where it's going to end."

The bitter finality in his voice had panic flaring. She struggled against her bonds. Ben was coming, and he would be in danger, too. "How did you know it was us who had video of you? We saw you run off."

"I always hang around for a while and watch my fires. I saw y'all come down off the roof."

Of course he'd stayed to watch, she thought. Typical firebug behavior.

"How did y'all know I would be there?"

"We didn't."

"But you knew there would be a fire there. How?"

Because I saw the whole thing beforehand. Aloud,

she said, "Things will go easier for you if you turn yourself in."

"I'm not turning myself in, and you won't be doing it again, either." He moved to one of the over-sized burgundy chairs at the foot of the couch and bent to pick up something from the floor.

"So this is about me doing the right thing and turning you in when you were setting all those fires?"

Walking past her, he carefully set a small food storage container on the end table closest to Cass, then shoved his face into hers. "Being disloyal isn't the right thing. You took me out of commission. Now I'm doing the same thing to you."

His words roused a greasy feeling in her stomach. Had he spent the last three years in prison thinking up ways to hurt her? "So it *was* you who tried to kill me at that hotel fire?"

"I still don't know how you survived that beam falling on you. The paper said you died and came back to life. What a crock."

Hoping to think of a way to convince him to discard his plan, she tried to keep him talking. "That was you I saw there, wasn't it? You wore turnout gear, and no one even noticed you didn't belong."

He gave a smug smile as he eased between their father's tan recliner and the end table to the wall covered with awards.

"The night you left that plaque at the firehouse, how did you know I wasn't there?"

"I was watching you. Saw that fire investigator drop you off then come back to pick you up."

That was because she'd told him about finding the

plaque. Her stomach knotted. "How did you manage to get in without anyone noticing?"

"I waited until they were watching TV then snuck behind the fire engine and went upstairs. I left through your bunk room window."

He gestured toward the many plaques and mounted medals on the wall.

"What did you get when you turned me in? Some kind of commendation? Why isn't it here on Daddy's wall of fame?"

"You know you can't get away with this." Cass pulled against her bonds, the tape biting into her wrists. "You'll go back to prison. Even longer this time."

"I'm not going back to prison, little sister," he snarled. "Once I get that video, I'm outta here. With no loose ends."

He was still planning to kill her, she realized. How had things gone so wrong? Heartsick, fear growing, her throat tightened. "Stop this, please. You said you didn't kill Officer Giles, but you did kill a child at that department store. That's murder, Lee."

He slipped the policeman's gun into the waistband of his grimy jeans, gesturing at a dark walnut plaque. "Do you remember when he got this Distinguished Service Award? Right after I washed out of the fire academy. Good timing, huh?"

"Lee." She knew he blamed their father for almost everything. Lee had never wanted to be a firefighter, but he had lacked the self-confidence to tell gruff, blustering Mike Hollister so. As a result, her brother's resentment had grown deeper every year. "You can get away without involving anyone else."

"As soon as that fire investigator gets here with the camera, I'll be gone for good."

Cass wanted to scream from the frustration and fear of being unable to keep Ben away and safe.

Suddenly an image of flames shot through her mind. Staggered by the unexpected flash, she tried to fight, but she barely had time to acknowledge it before she was yanked into the vision.

This one was different. The blaze was already out. Smoke was funneling out through a ragged hole in the ceiling. Wood and glass littered the floor. Furniture and walls had crumbled into crackling piles of ash. Her gaze scanned a scorched leather sofa, a charred fabric recliner. Her dad's recliner. She was looking at her own living room! She saw Lee, then the vision ended.

Dazed, she blinked. The agony in her palms had her hands clenching into fists. Why had she seen the scene of a fire that had already burned?

"Hey!"

Lee's voice startled her out of her thoughts. He narrowed his eyes. "Did you just black out?"

"No."

"What's wrong with you?"

"Nothing." Her hands throbbed, but the pain was already fading.

After a long moment, Lee turned back to the awards, touching them in turn. "Meritorious service award. Twenty-five-year service award. Firefighter of the Year—twice."

He removed a light oak plaque distinguished with a brass OCFD badge. "Fire Chief's Award."

Making a sound of disgust, he came over and opened the plastic storage container he'd set down near her and removed a dull white jelly-like cube.

What was it? Cass wondered, her emotions zipping from anger to fear and back.

He carefully pressed the pliable material to the brass plate engraved with their father's name. From his left pocket, he took a slender metal cylinder about two inches long and crimped at one end.

Apprehension clawed through her.

With a small smile, he stuck the metal piece into the gelatinous substance. "Explosive."

Explosive? Cass thought frantically. So was that metal thing a blasting cap? It must be, although it looked unlike any of the few she had seen.

"Made it myself from bleach and salt substitute. Slick, huh?"

Suddenly she understood why there hadn't been a burning fire in her vision. Because it wasn't a fire that would destroy her house. It was a bomb. Her stomach turned. She didn't know her brother anymore, if she ever had. She fought against the band of tape around her wrists. The adhesive rubbed her skin raw.

"I just can't figure out how y'all managed to get to that fire before it even started. Like you already knew where it would be."

She had, but she was not telling him about her visions. No way. "Just lucky."

"Not so lucky now, huh?"

Ben would be here soon, and Lee would kill him, too, she thought. Nauseous, her skin peppered with cold sweat, she realized she'd made an awful mistake leaving Ben the first time. And she'd nearly done it again. Now she might never get the chance to tell him how wrong she had been.

Lee centered the plaque in the seat of their father's well-used chair. The corduroy fabric was frayed in places, and Cass knew the chair should be thrown out, but she kept it for sentimental reasons.

A sound came from the kitchen. The groan of a floorboard. Oh, no! Ben.

Lee's gaze shot to the dining area. "Ah, you're here, Investigator."

Cass figured Ben had tried to sneak in and the stupid floorboard had creaked. It had always creaked. Her brother would know immediately the noise wasn't caused by anything except another person.

She couldn't bear to think that Ben was about to be killed because of her.

"Get in here or I'm going to hurt her," Lee demanded.

"He can leave the camera for you," Cass argued. "He doesn't have to come in here."

"Yeah, he does." Lee raised his voice. "Investigator, if I don't see you in three seconds, I'll shoot her."

Ben stepped into sight, and Cass nearly cried.

He glanced at her, concern dark in his eyes. "You okay?"

She nodded.

"Let her go, Hollister," Ben said. "I have what you want."

"Lee," Cass begged. "Let him leave. Please."

"Shut up!" Her brother's gaze swung to Ben. "Where is it?"

Ben held up the video camera as he moved into the living room.

"This doesn't have to end badly," he said.

"It isn't going to end badly for me." Gesturing with the gun he'd stolen, Lee directed the other man toward the middle of the room. "Walk over, put the camera on the coffee table and step back."

"He's planning to kill both of us," Cass said.

A muscle flexed in Ben's stony jaw, but he did as Lee ordered, edging between the leather chairs at the foot of the couch. Angling his body, he kept both Cass and her brother in view.

She tried to communicate with her eyes that she'd had a vision. Staring intently at Ben, she lifted her hands, turning her palms up as much as the tape biting into her wrists allowed.

Ben read the urgency and fear in her eyes. She was trying to tell him something. When she made a show of looking at her palms, he knew she'd had a vision. "Here?" he asked.

"Yes. It's not a fire."

Lee looked from Cass to Ben. "What are y'all talking about?"

Not a fire? Scanning the room, Ben tried to figure out how Cass's brother planned to get rid of the place and them along with it. His gaze snagged on the award resting in the chair, and he cursed under his breath.

That was plastic explosive with a blasting cap! But there was no fuse attached. If Lee wasn't using conventional means, such as a match or a lighter, how was he going to set it off?

The other man slid something out of his pocket. A red dot of light skipped around on the carpet.

Alarmed, Ben realized the SOB had a laser detonator and could use it from outside, a good distance from the house. Adrenaline spiking his blood, he moved on sheer instinct. He flipped his wrist, firing the video camera like a Frisbee right into Lee's face. The unexpected blow was enough to make the other man flinch and stumble, then fall backward to the floor.

Ben wasted no time. Kicking aside the coffee table, he grabbed Cass and threw her over his shoulder in a fireman's hold, then headed for the nearest exit—a sliding glass door leading out to the covered patio. Shoving it open, he ran as fast as possible while carrying her. He crossed the yard, heading for the back chain-link fence.

A muscle cramped sharply in Ben's side. Glaring evening sunlight stung his eyes. Cass stayed still, helping him keep his balance. Sweat trickled down his temple, into his eyes.

An explosion rocked the house.

Deafened by the thunderous blast, Ben threw himself to the ground, turning so that his shoulder, rather than Cass's, hit the summer-baked dirt. He rolled, putting her beneath him.

As another explosion shook the earth, he curled his body around Cass. Debris rained down. Fiery sparks, wood and shards of glass pelted his forearms and neck.

Then the boom began to fade. As the buzzing in his ears dimmed, he heard the crackle of flames. Heat and smoke rolled toward them like a tide.

He got to his knees, checking over his shoulder. The center of the house had collapsed in on itself. While the firefighters who'd trailed him rolled up and trained water on the structure to drown any burning embers, Ben hurriedly helped Cass to her feet and worked the tape off her wrists.

She was shaking, her red-rimmed eyes huge in her pale face. She gripped his hand. "Lee?"

No one could have survived that explosion, and Ben was damn glad Cass hadn't been the one inside. Grimly, he shook his head.

They would never know if Lee had accidentally triggered the detonator or not.

She choked back a sob and grasped his shoulder as he knelt to unbind her ankles.

The paramedics checked them both and released them. Then they gave their statements to the incident commander, the fire investigator and the OCPD detective who would work the case together, because a death was involved.

As Cass stood alone under a tree, she hurt over the loss of her home and her brother, and over what her brother had become, but she knew that in reality she'd lost him long ago.

She looked up, and her gaze tracked Ben to where he stood talking to the incident commander. She caught his eye, but he quickly looked away.

Afraid she'd lost him for good, she walked over toward the ladder truck where he stood with a burly red-faced man, hoping she wasn't too late to tell him she'd been wrong to try to leave again.

She wanted to rush over and hug him, but she wasn't sure what kind of reception she would get. Her hands trembled as she asked, "Can we talk?"

Heat flared in his eyes before they shuttered against her. "Do we have something to talk about?"

"I hope so."

At her words, Cass saw a vulnerability in his eyes that stunned her. Until that moment, she hadn't realized how unsure he was of her. He hadn't expected her to stay.

The fact that he believed she had walked away again left her with a hollow ache.

Tentatively, she reached out and took his hand, encouraged when he didn't pull away. Still, he wore the same reserve he had when visiting her in the hospital. She caught a whiff of his clean sharp scent beneath lingering smoke.

"I'm sorry about your brother."

"Thank you," she said, her voice cracking. "But I really lost him a long time ago. I was afraid I'd lost you, too. I'm so sorry, Ben. I was such an idiot."

His gaze sharpened.

"You were right. What happened when we were in bed made me panic. I couldn't imagine going through that again or putting you through it. When I said I couldn't be with you, I thought I was protecting you."

A muscle flexed in his jaw as he stared at her skeptically.

Her voice thickened. "I didn't realize how deeply I was hurting you."

She wanted him to say something, but he remained quiet, his expression inscrutable. Every long silent second scraped against her nerves like a blade.

Had she completely ruined things between them? How could she convince him that she meant to stay? "I—I know I made a mistake when I left eight months ago. I knew how I felt, but I wasn't ready to accept it then. Am I too late? Can you forgive me?"

He said nothing. Dread knotted her stomach. "Ben?"

He caught her hand and pulled her around to the other side of the ladder truck. Hidden from view, he backed her into the vehicle. "Yes, I can forgive you. And I'm sorry, too. About what I said earlier. Or, actually, the way I said it. I realize the caveman approach might not have been the best way to handle things."

She thought of how she'd hurt him, how she'd nearly lost him. All she wanted was to kiss him, but there was something she had to say first. "Your approach was better than mine."

He braced one arm over her head and curved the other around her waist, fingers caressing her lower back, heating her blood. "I thought I'd run you off. Screwed up everything."

She looked into his eyes and felt her heart catch. She didn't want him to doubt her ever again.

"I was afraid to trust my feelings before, but not now. I love you."

His eyes flared hotly. "Does that make you want to run?"

"No. It makes me want to stay."

He stilled. "No matter what?"

"No matter what."

His hand flattened on the small of her back, urging her into him. "Even if you see another fire?"

"Even if." She was disappointed that he hadn't said he loved her, but she knew it might take him a while to believe she was sticking around. "About that. The vision I had in my house was of a bomb, not a fire. The only thing those fires and the bomb have in common is Lee. I never saw blazes started by anyone else, so perhaps I saw the things I did because Lee's my brother. Maybe whatever happened to me at the hotel fire happened because I was supposed to stop him."

"So you think the visions might stop?" Ben pulled her closer.

"I hope they will. It's just a theory, and it may be completely wrong. But if I do still have these episodes, I don't want to face them without you. Although if one hits during sex, I'll probably freak out again. At least the first few times."

"That's okay, as long as you don't take off."

"I won't. Ever again."

The tension drained out of him. His lips drifted over the curve of her cheek. "I love you, too."

A sense of rightness she'd never known before warmed her. Her feelings for Ben were different than anything she'd felt for any other man. Deeper. *More*.

"Say it again," she said dreamily.

He nudged her chin up with one knuckle, blue eyes burning into hers. "I love you."

"It's a good thing, because I'm not going any-where. Think you can deal with that?"

He laughed, murmuring against her lips, "Oh, yeah."

Here's a sneak peek at
THE CEO'S CHRISTMAS PROPOSITION,
the first in USA TODAY *bestselling author*
Merline Lovelace's HOLIDAYS ABROAD *trilogy*
coming in November 2008.

American Devon McShay is about to get the
Christmas surprise of a lifetime when she meets
her new client, sexy billionaire Caleb Logan,
for the very first time.

Silhouette
Desire

Available November 2008

Her breath whistled out in a sigh of relief when he exited Customs. Devon recognized him right away from the newspaper and magazine articles her friend and partner Sabrina had looked up during her frantic prep work.

Caleb John Logan, Jr. Thirty-one. Six-two. With jet-black hair, laser-blue eyes and a linebacker's shoulders under his charcoal-gray cashmere overcoat. His jaw-dropping good looks didn't score him any points with Devon. She'd learned the hard way not to trust handsome heartbreakers like Cal Logan.

But he was a client. An important one. And she was willing to give someone who'd served a hitch in the marines before earning a B.S. from the University of Oregon, an MBA from Stanford and his first million at the ripe old age of twenty-six the benefit of the doubt.

Right up until he spotted the hot-pink pashmina, that is.

Devon knew the flash of color was more visible than the sign she held up with his name on it. So she wasn't surprised when Logan picked her out of the crowd and cut in her direction. She'd just plastered on her best businesswoman smile when he whipped an arm around her waist. The next moment she was sprawled against his cashmere-covered chest.

"Hello, brown eyes."

Swooping down, he covered her mouth with his.

Sheer astonishment kept Devon rooted to the spot for a few seconds while her mind whirled chaotically. Her first thought was that her client had downed a few too many drinks during the long flight. Her second, that he'd mistaken the kind of escort and consulting services her company provided. Her third shoved everything else out of her head.

The man could kiss!

His mouth moved over hers with a skill that ignited sparks at a half dozen flash points throughout her body. Devon hadn't experienced that kind of spontaneous combustion in a while. A *long* while.

The sparks were still popping when she pushed off his chest, only now they fueled a flush of anger.

"Do you always greet women you don't know with a lip-lock, Mr. Logan?"

A smile crinkled the skin at the corners of his eyes. "As a matter of fact, I don't. That was from Don."

"Huh?"

"He said he owed you one from New Year's Eve two years ago and made me promise to deliver it."

She stared up at him in total incomprehension. Logan hooked a brow and attempted to prompt a nonexistent memory.

"He abandoned you at the Waldorf. Five minutes before midnight. To deliver twins."

"I don't have a clue who or what you're..."

Understanding burst like a water balloon.

"Wait a sec. Are you talking about Sabrina's old boyfriend? Your buddy, who's now an ob-gyn doc?"

It was Logan's turn to look startled. He recovered faster than Devon had, though. His smile widened into a rueful grin.

"I take it you're not Sabrina Russo."

"No, Mr. Logan, I am *not*."

* * * * *

Be sure to look for
THE CEO'S CHRISTMAS PROPOSITION
by Merline Lovelace.
Available in November 2008
wherever books are sold,
including most bookstores, supermarkets,
drugstores and discount stores.

MERLINE LOVELACE

THE CEO'S CHRISTMAS PROPOSITION

After being stranded in Austria together
at Christmas, it takes only one kiss for
aerospace CEO Cal Logan to decide he wants
more than just a business relationship with
Devon McShay. But when Cal's credibility is
questioned, he has to fight to clear his name,
and to get Devon to trust her heart.

**Available November
wherever books are sold.**

Holidays Abroad

Always Powerful, Passionate and Provocative.

MIRA®

The chilling
Flynn Brothers trilogy
from bestselling author

HEATHER GRAHAM

**SAVE
$1.⁰⁰**

DEADLY NIGHT
DEADLY HARVEST
DEADLY GIFT

Coming October 2008.

**SAVE
$1.⁰⁰** on the purchase price of one
book in the Flynn Brothers trilogy
by Heather Graham.

Offer valid from September 30, 2008, to December 31, 2008.
Redeemable at participating retail outlets. Limit one coupon per purchase.
Valid in the U.S. and Canada only.

52608517

5 65373 00076 2   (8100) 0 11566

REQUEST YOUR FREE BOOKS!

2 FREE NOVELS PLUS 2 FREE GIFTS!

Silhouette®

nocturne™

Dramatic and Sensual Tales of Paranormal Romance.

YES! Please send me 2 FREE Silhouette® Nocturne™ novels and my 2 FREE gifts (gifts are worth about $10). After receiving them, if I don't wish to receive any more books, I can return the shipping statement marked "cancel." If I don't cancel, I will receive 4 brand-new novels every other month and be billed just $4.47 per book in the U.S. or $4.99 per book in Canada, plus 25¢ shipping and handling per book plus applicable taxes, if any*. That's a savings of about 15% off the cover price! I understand that accepting the 2 free books and gifts places me under no obligation to buy anything. I can always return a shipment and cancel at any time. Even if I never buy another book from Silhouette, the two free books and gifts are mine to keep forever.

238 SDN ELS4 338 SDN ELXG

Name	(PLEASE PRINT)

Address	Apt. #

City	State/Prov.	Zip/Postal Code

Signature (if under 18, a parent or guardian must sign)

Mail to the **Silhouette Reader Service:**
IN U.S.A.: P.O. Box 1867, Buffalo, NY 14240-1867
IN CANADA: P.O. Box 609, Fort Erie, Ontario L2A 5X3

Not valid to current subscribers of Silhouette Nocturne books.

Want to try two free books from another line?
Call 1-800-873-8635 or visit www.morefreebooks.com.

* Terms and prices subject to change without notice. N.Y. residents add applicable sales tax. Canadian residents will be charged applicable provincial taxes and GST. Offer not valid in Quebec. This offer is limited to one order per household. All orders subject to approval. Credit or debit balances in a customer's account(s) may be offset by any other outstanding balance owed by or to the customer. Please allow 4 to 6 weeks for delivery. Offer available while quantities last.

Your Privacy: Silhouette is committed to protecting your privacy. Our Privacy Policy is available online at www.eHarlequin.com or upon request from the Reader Service. From time to time we make our lists of customers available to reputable third parties who may have a product or service of interest to you. If you would prefer we not share your name and address, please check here. ☐

SN08R

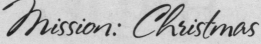

Silhouette®

nocturne™

COMING NEXT MONTH

#51 ENEMY LOVER • Bonnie Vanak

Jaimie Walsh had once believed Damien Marcel was responsible for the death of her brother—and she'd tried to kill the Pack leader to avenge that murder. But when she failed, and her evil cohorts turned on her by inciting a spell that would turn her to stone, Jaimie found herself at her enemy's mercy. For although he had every reason to distrust Jaimie, Damien knew she was his chosen mate, and he would stop at nothing to save her life....

#52 WINTER KISSED • Michael Hauf, Vivi Anna

Warm up with two tales of sizzling romance. In "A Kiss of Frost," Jal Frosti is a Norse-god assassin with a problem. The mortal woman he's been sent to kill provides a sense of warmth he's never known. But will Kate Wilson's affection help him find love for the first time? Or will Jal have to choose between the woman he loves and his duty as a god?

In "Ice Bound," Dr. Darien Calder finds himself discovering first hand the Japanese legend of the ice maiden when Yuki rescues him from a snowdrift. Will his love be enough to melt the ice around her heart?

SNCNM1008